Accidental Runaway Groom

CARRIE ANN
NEW YORK TIMES BESTSELLING AUTHOR
RYAN

ACCIDENTAL RUNAWAY GROOM

A CLOVER LAKE / MONTGOMERY INK LEGACY CROSSOVER ROMANCE

CLOVER LAKE

BOOK TWO

CARRIE ANN RYAN

Accidental Runaway Groom
By: Carrie Ann Ryan
© 2025 Carrie Ann Ryan

Cover Art by Sweet N Spicy Designs

For Brandi.
Still blaming you.

Accidental Runaway Groom

CHAPTER ONE

Sharp

The main stipulations that I'd given my brothers and friends when I'd gotten engaged was that my bachelor party could *not* go off the rails. There would be no heavy drinking, no strippers, no obscene, ridiculous, out-of-hand event. I didn't want to be ashamed of what I did the next morning. Making sure that Jo still enjoyed being with me and wasn't ashamed of my actions, was kind of an important part of getting married. Her being embarrassed because I had stayed out too late the night before the wedding would not be a good way to start off our marriage.

My brothers, Ewan and Galen, as well as my sister Gwen had all agreed that being an idiot when it came to a bachelor party wasn't in the cards. In fact, when my elder brother Ewan had gotten married to his wife Livvy, we hadn't had a ridiculous bachelor party, which would leave everybody with hangovers, regret, and not a little bit of nausea.

Instead, we'd gone out for a sunset ride, had a single drink with our dad, from one of the single barrels that he liked so much, and then come back to hang out with Ewan's stepdaughter, Amelia.

Maybe that made us old, or even a little non-traditional, but it wasn't as if we didn't hang out all the time anyway. And heavy drinking had never really been our thing.

Even my younger brother Galen had agreed, although he had wanted to go a little more exuberant than we had with Ewan. Probably because I wasn't a dad, and we were slightly younger.

However, agreements were made, and a small yet tasteful bachelor party had been planned.

So why did I taste vomit on my tongue, and my head felt as if somebody had driven a nail right into my temple? And not just a tiny nail. No, one of those ragged ones that got overheated when you hit it too many times. Or maybe even a screw. The same type of screw that got too hot and turned practically magnetic and weirdly sharp because you were drilling into a stud and decided to strip the damn thing.

Yes, one of each dug deep into my temples. That was exactly what was happening.

What the hell had happened the night before?

It was morning, right? It had to be.

I swallowed hard and realized I hadn't actually opened my eyes yet.

Oh yes, the day was going well.

Today.

My wedding day.

Well, fuck.

With trepidation slithering over my skin, I pried open one eyelid and promptly shut it.

Dear God, who invented the sun, and why was it so bright?

I swallowed back that dryness again, jagged shards of glass tearing my throat, and forced both eyes open this time.

I was a cattle rancher, a cowboy to some, and had ridden bulls when I had been younger and far more stupid. After all, my frontal lobe hadn't quite been developed yet.

I could handle a wee bit of sunlight.

The sun glared back at me—despite the increasing number of clouds rolling their way into the horizon—and I put one hand on my leather upholstery and forced myself into seated position. Why was I in one of the family's old trucks?

Not my new 4x4 with the deep bucket seats that had the best heater in the world during winter and the cooling bands for a hot summer. No, this was one of the older trucks that had the bench seat, so I had been practically sprawled over it, and I had no idea how I had gotten here.

I ran my hand through my hair and winced at the crick in my neck. Where the hell was I? And why did I have zero memory of how I'd gotten here? I swallowed hard, trying to wet my mouth as it was oddly dry. I blinked again and realized that since the sun shone far too brightly in my eyes, I was at least facing east, and on one of the main farm roads off the highway that led to the McBride Ranch and lands, but other than that, I was still a little groggy on everything that had happened.

I tried to find my phone and cursed. I wore my jeans from last night, that much I remembered, but I had no keys, no wallet, no phone. Panic increasing now, I opened the glove compartment, didn't find it there, and began to search the cab of the truck. Nope. Nothing.

How the hell had I gotten here? And what the hell was happening? I opened the door, the rusted metal screeching ever so slightly to the point that it felt like it jingled those nails and screws right back into my temples.

"What happened last night?" I muttered as I gingerly stepped out of the cab, my boots pressing into the packed dirt beneath my feet.

I was somehow pulled to the side of the road, and sleeping in my truck, without any identifying markers or way of getting home and/or contacting someone. That's when a sliver of a memory hit.

The entire mess of my unknown surroundings and headache had nothing to do with my bachelor party.

No, this had happened *after*.

We'd gone on the same ride we had done for Ewan, had a single glass of bourbon, courtesy of Ewan's very rich friend, and had ended up back at our respective homes.

Each of the McBride siblings owned a piece of land that was all part of the main McBride Ranch.

Even my uncles had their own space far out to the west, and it was separated between their four sons each.

Well, it had been. When we'd lost one of my cousins a few years ago, things had shifted a bit, but other than that, the family was pretty spread out, and all worked together on their own ranches.

I wasn't currently on McBride property, but I had been the night before.

And then I had gone back to my cabin, knowing I would have a long day today—my wedding day—and had one more drink before calling it an early night.

Then I didn't remember a damn thing.

Until now.

There were vague recollections of me falling asleep in my armchair, that bourbon tasting slightly funny, and then being carried over somebody's broad shoulder into the truck.

That's all I could really remember, and frankly, it almost sounded like a dream. A memory that I wanted to fit into the holes that were feeling like Swiss cheese at this point.

My brothers wouldn't do this. They wouldn't drug me and kidnap me the day before my wedding. Well, they didn't really like Jo, or understand why we were getting married, but they wouldn't hurt me. Right?

Dear God. I was going to be late to my own wedding. Because Jo had wanted an early morning wedding, so we could spend the rest of the afternoon celebrating before heading off to our honeymoon in Aruba on an evening flight.

I was going to miss my own wedding. Jo would be the jilted bride, and I would be the runaway groom.

I was in so much trouble.

Hands on hips, I glared into the distance, trying to figure out how long it would take to walk to the main house. I couldn't walk to the church from here, as that was even farther, but now that I had my bearings, I could make it happen.

By tomorrow.

"Shit."

The sound of an engine cut through my worry, and I turned to see a shiny SUV making its way up the farm road, not quite speeding, but it didn't look familiar. It wasn't like we owned this road, but now that I knew where I was, and that I was closer to the ranch than I had originally thought. And that meant whoever was driving had to be part of the farm. Right? Or maybe they were my kidnapper.

Alarm shot through me for an instant, until I told myself I was an idiot.

Clouds began to roll in as I waved my arms, trying to get this person's attention. Hopefully they would take a stranger, if they didn't know me, because I was about to need to hitchhike to my own wedding.

I looked up and glared at the now darkening clouds.

Rain was supposed to be good luck on a wedding day from what I could vaguely remember. The groom not showing up however, that didn't sound like good luck.

With a curse, I lifted my arms again, ignoring the increasing wind that seemed to come with those clouds. This could not be happening. And yet, it was. I'd get to the bottom of it, and hope whoever thought this practical joke was funny would get their comeuppance later, but for now, I needed to get to my family.

To Jo.

I waved down the car again just as the first drops of rain fell. "Lovely," I growled.

As the next drop came, and then the deluge of rain decided to follow, I pushed my dark hair back from my face and hoped that my square jaw, broad shoulders, and glaring blue eyes wouldn't scare off whoever the hell was finally coming closer.

The SUV's lights turned on as the rain began to pour in earnest, and finally the driver pulled over to the side.

Thank God for friendly people who didn't mind hitchhikers.

"Please don't be a serial killer," I muttered.

The formerly packed ground beneath my feet began to turn to mud as I stomped my way through in my work boots, and made my way to the passenger side of the SUV.

When the window opened, I swallowed hard, not recognizing the woman in front of me but still a little confused. Because while I had never seen her before, she had to be one of the most beautiful women I had ever laid eyes on.

She had white-blond hair with hot pink strips, bright blue eyes, and luscious lips.

Not that I should be paying attention to her lips. This was a stranger. And I was supposed to be getting married soon. The only person's lips I should be thinking about were Jo's. The one who I liked. No, loved. Right? Well, we were friendly. And we enjoyed each other's company. Those were some of the reasons that we were getting married, and it didn't have to be the head over heels love at first sight that Ewan and Livvy had.

Why I sounded so confrontational in my own head, I didn't know.

"Hey there," I said after a moment, hoping I didn't sound serial killer-like.

"Hi." The hesitancy in her voice struck me, but she smiled, and I swallowed hard. Then I nearly tilted my head back to wet my mouth with the rain that continued to pour down on me. I must look ridiculous, but I didn't care. Well, I did. I just needed to get to my damn wedding.

"I would ask if everything's okay, but it clearly isn't. Is your truck broken down?"

"Not precisely," I said after a moment.

Her eyes widened, and that's when I realized that she had one of those keychain canisters in her hand that was probably pepper spray or mace.

That was pretty damn smart, considering she was a woman traveling alone, and getting pepper spray to the face would just be a cherry on top of my what the fuck Sunday.

"My name is Sharp. My ranch is down the way. I just need to get back to my house. And my truck." I paused, wondering what the hell I was supposed to say. "And to my wedding. I'm getting married today," I added quickly, though the light tone I was going for wasn't anywhere in existence. Instead, I just sounded grumpy.

I would blame the rain.

"Oh. Sharp McBride? Are you Ewan's brother?"

"You know Ewan?" I asked, slightly confused.

"I am Livvy's cousin, Jamie. One of the Montgomerys."

My shoulders nearly relaxed as a smile spread on my face. Considering how my day was already going, I hadn't realized I could smile. "One of the many Montgomery cousins?"

Her eyes filled with laughter. "That's it. And I can't believe I'm still leaving you out in the rain. Let me unlock the door for you so you can hop in. Do you need anything from your truck?"

Relieved, I shook my head as I opened the door and then looked down at her expensive leather seat. "I don't have anything on me, and I'm going to ruin your seats."

"Well, I don't have a towel with me, so get in. It's fine. It will clean. Or my dad will help me figure out something. He's very handy that way."

I didn't know which branch of the family tree Jamie was part of, but I did know that most of the older generation Montgomery men were all built and could probably break me over their knee. It didn't matter that I was a sturdy rancher, the Montgomerys were something fierce.

"I really should've recognized you. After all, I know Ewan, and while I wasn't going to your wedding today, I'm heading up to help Livvy with a few things on the ranch and was planning on getting there right when she was leaving. That way I could set up. But wow. Okay. I have so many questions."

"I have a few myself," I said, my voice low. "Do you mind driving to the church? Because now that I look at the time, I'm not going to have enough of it in order to get to the house first."

"Oh. Okay. I can totally do that. As long as you tell me how to get there." She gave me a sheepish look, as she looked through the side mirrors, and turned on her blinker to get back on the road. "Will you be okay leaving your truck back there?"

"It's one of the work trucks, and yes. I'll have somebody come by and get it. If we figure out where the hell the keys are."

Her eyes widened. "The keys aren't there? Then how did you get out here?"

One of many questions that started to add a

worry to my gut that felt like stomach acid. "I have no idea."

"I'm confused."

"Take the next right. And I am too. I found myself on this side of the world, and I have no idea how I got there." For some reason, I told her the exact truth. Everything that I remembered anyway. I didn't even know this Jamie Montgomery, but apparently, she was going to be the one who I told everything to.

Which didn't make any sense, but then again, nothing did today.

"Sharp, you need to call the police."

I shook my head, not liking my reaction to my name coming off those lips. "No. I'll figure that out later. It's Clover Lake, there's not too many of us. It was probably a practical joke by one of Jo's brothers."

She gave me a weird look before going back to paying attention to the road. As it was still raining out, and her knuckles were turning white with how hard she was gripping the steering wheel, she must be freaking out.

I was freaking out too. I liked Jo well enough. I hated her brothers. Hated her family. However, they were one of the neighboring ranches, and being on good terms with them kept us safe and in business. And it would be good for my family, for my relationship with Jo to go to the next level.

Falling in line and making sure that the ranch ran smoothly was what I did. It was just easier to do so. I didn't love Jo, not yet. But I liked her well enough. And even if I didn't love her, that was no excuse to miss a wedding. Especially since her father would probably have his shotgun handy.

"I wonder if they're out looking for you. They have to be worried. Here. What am I thinking? My phone is in the cubby. I have Ewan's number in there, if you want to text him."

I pinched the bridge of my nose. "That's smart. Thanks."

I pulled out the phone and cursed. This wedding was going to be the end of me. "If you had signal."

"I don't have signal?" she asked, her voice high-pitched.

I understood her worry as she was a woman driving in the middle of nowhere alone, but since this was home, I was used to it. On a normal day. "It happens out here with some of the storms. We are in the middle of nowhere."

"It's Wyoming, I just assumed the whole state

was the middle of nowhere," she teased, still sounding a little alarmed.

"You say that as someone who lives in Colorado."

"In Denver. A metropolis. Yes, the mountains are there to remind you that nature exists, but it's not this." She gestured towards the stormy horizon where you couldn't see much, and I sighed.

"No, this is no Denver. Thank you though. We'll get there, and everything will be fine."

She risked a glance at me, and I realized I was staring at her. I should probably stop that. "Congratulations on the wedding though."

"If it still happens," I mumbled.

Her eyes widened, but she didn't say anything.

"It'll all work out. This wedding. Jo. Figuring out what the fuck happened. Pardon my language."

"I've probably cursed more than you, you're fucking fine," she teased.

My lips twitched. "Good to know."

"Yeah."

We sat in silence for the rest of the trip, an awkwardness settling in. Because I had no idea what the hell was going on. How I had gotten out here, what the hell this feeling was in my chest.

Who was Livvy's cousin, and why the hell did I have to meet her now?

Not that it mattered.

We pulled into the church's parking lot, and the rain came down even harder.

"Rain is supposed to be good luck for weddings, right?" she asked, her voice slightly shaky.

I met her gaze and raised a brow. "Sure. That's what I was thinking earlier, but this seems like a bit much."

She let out a long breath, her eyes still on mine. "You should probably get in there. Just in case."

My throat tightened. Was I making a mistake? Probably. But it was my mistake to make. Jo was counting on me. And I didn't back away from commitments—even ones I didn't want to make. "Yeah. My wedding that I'm well over an hour late for."

Jamie winced. "Well, that's not good."

"No. It really isn't."

"Good luck."

"I think I'm going to need it." I turned, and for some reason reached out to squeeze her hand. "Thank you, Jamie Montgomery."

She looked down where we touched before she

smiled up at me. "You're welcome, Sharp McBride. Now go get married."

"On it."

And with that, I jumped out of her SUV, ran through the pouring rain, and made my way inside the church. Both doors were slightly stuck, so I pushed them open together, bending at the waist and realized I probably resembled Aragon trying to make his way into the hall, but from the daggers that Jo's mother glared at me from the side, I wasn't going to get the same reception.

"Where the hell were you?" Jo's father snapped, as my father moved alongside him.

Angus McBride visibly sighed. "Oh thank God. Your brothers were out looking for you, and we found your phone in your house, but we couldn't…" He shook his head. "And your truck was there too. We've been so worried."

My mother practically pushed my dad to the side to hug me tightly, ignoring how wet I was. "I'm so glad that you're okay."

"Okay? He's not going to be okay for long. He ran out on my baby girl," Jo's father roared.

Everybody began talking at once, screaming at each other, and I put my two fingers to my mouth and whistled sharply. "I'll explain later, I'm sorry I'm late, I couldn't help it."

"That's rich," one of Jo's brothers snarled.

And then I looked up, ignoring everyone else, as Jo came down the aisle, her long and fluffy dress billowing as she stepped.

"Jo. It's not what you think."

"You bastard." I didn't block the first punch as she slammed her fist into my cheek. She'd been trained by her brothers and could hit like a prize fighter. I did, however, block the punch that came from her brother.

"Okay, that's enough of that," Ewan said as he shifted toward us and pulled one of Jo's brothers away.

Jo moved forward again, her eyes bright with fury…and something else I couldn't name. "You left me!"

This was going from bad to worse. "I didn't. I promise. Just give me a minute to explain and we can get through this." Not that I knew exactly how I'd ended up in this position. There was something fishy going on and I couldn't put my finger on it.

"You left me for her." Jo pointed a shaky hand behind me, and I nearly closed my eyes and prayed.

Well hell.

I turned, knowing exactly who I would see. A wet and bedraggled Jamie stood there, hands wringing in front of her, and her eyes wide.

"You cheated on me!" Jo screeched.

"I did not. It's not what you think," I repeated. This time Jo's father punched me on my other cheek, and then my dad was there pinning Jo's father to the ground. I hadn't even seen him move. Everybody shouted at once, pulling off boutonnières and kicking, and even my mother had Jo's mother in a headlock.

Jamie came closer, as if to help stop this, as Jo's uncle threw his fist out to punch. I caught it with one hand so it wouldn't hit her and pulled the man's arm down. Then Jamie put her fingers to her mouth and whistled even louder than I had.

Everybody stopped and stared at her.

She blinked at us, as if surprised to be the center of attention after that whistle. "I found him on the side of the road. We just met. I have no idea what happened, but all Sharp wanted to do was get here to his wedding. I promise."

"And who the hell are you?" Jo sobbed.

"My cousin," Livvy said pointedly as she wrapped her arm around her drenched cousin. "And

I would love it if you stopped using that tone when it comes to my family."

There was a reason I liked to Livvy.

"The wedding is off. I can't believe you did this to me. You humiliated me."

I just stared at Jo and realized that the only embarrassment came from the fact that my family had ended up in a fistfight with Jo's.

I stood there, confused as hell, and then met my father's gaze. He gave me a slight nod, and I realized that maybe he'd known all along that I didn't love Jo. Or perhaps I was reading too much into that look. I opened my mouth to say something, anything, but instead Jo just pushed past me, sobbing, and ran right into the arms of William, confusing all of us.

William, the former deputy who'd lost his job thanks to a few too many fistfights, who now owned a local tractor supply and repair company, held Jo to his chest and glared at me, and I realized I'd been set up.

Jo hadn't wanted to be a runaway bride, so instead she'd made me the runaway groom.

The cheater.

The backstabber.

And no matter what I said, nothing would make it better.

I turned on my heel, nodded at my family, and walked away, leaving this mess, and one of the worst decisions I had ever made in my life, behind.

And when the small tap of heels behind me echoed throughout the church, I realized that Jamie was there, tossing me her keys. "You kind of need a getaway car," she whispered.

My lips quirked into a smile, and I tilted my imaginary hat in thanks, before leaving the church.

Running away from the wedding that never should have taken place in the first place.

In a town as small as Clover Lake, this was only going to get bad before it got better.

Chapter Two

Jamie

6 Months Later

ARMS FULL OF MY NEPHEW, I ROCKED BEAU IN MY arms and smiled down at him. He proceeded to smile right back at me, and my eyes widened. "Okay, that's enough. He's all yours." I practically shoved Beau into my brother Colin's arms, as the stench of whatever had made Beau smile with such intensity hit my nostrils.

Colin gagged and glared at me as I took a few steps back. "I cannot believe you just did that."

"Finders keepers. I'm out. I do not deal with diapers."

"Seriously? With all the babies in our lives, you refuse to even touch a diaper?" Leif asked as he took his son from Colin's arms with the click of his tongue. "Come on, baby boy. Let's go change that diaper of yours. You smell like you made a big poop. Look at what you did! Good for you. Your system is doing the work!"

Beau made a squeaking noise, and I rolled my eyes as I met Colin's gaze. "He sounds so proud of his son's poop. When did Leif become that type of guy?"

"About the time that he became a father for the first time," Gideon answered as he walked into the living room with a cringe on his face. It most likely matched the one mine made since the scent hadn't quite dissipated. The youngest Montgomery son came forward and hugged me tightly, before doing the same to Colin.

I was the youngest of four. Technically. After all, Gideon was my twin. And while we weren't Montgomerys by blood, as Gideon and I had been adopted at birth by our parents, Gideon still looked more like my dad than Leif did sometimes.

My parents, Austin and Sierra Montgomery, were the eldest of the entire Montgomery crew. And considering there were so many of us, that was saying something. Leif was the oldest of my generation, and while technically our mom wasn't his birth mom, she'd been in his life since he was ten years old. Colin was the only one who technically had the genetics of both of our parents, but in reality, it didn't matter. The Montgomerys were all about family, and it didn't matter how you were blended into them.

Having three older brothers however, made for interesting times. And by interesting, I meant ridiculous.

After all, Leif had been seventeen when Gideon and I were born and had been on his way to Paris after graduation, and everything had changed, slightly cut short when he hadn't planned on it. We had been the surprise of a lifetime when it came to our parents.

I wanted to pull my hair out sometimes with how overprotective they were. My cousins were worse, because they enjoyed thinking of me as one of the babies, even though I wasn't the youngest cousin by far.

I was one of the shortest, and for some reason that led them to believe I needed the most help in just living at this point.

I didn't live with my parents, I had a nice apartment that I enjoyed, and I had full-time job—that happened to be with the Montgomery businesses, but most of us worked for them anyway—and I was doing well for myself. There was always a worried look when they glanced at me, and I didn't know what I had done to deserve it.

"I see my grandbaby is being a menace," my mom said as she wrapped her arm around my shoulder. I leaned into her hold, relaxing at the sight of her.

Sierra Montgomery was one of the most gorgeous women in the world, and I wasn't even a little biased in that. She had a little gray at her temples but loved to dye her hair as much as I did, so no one would ever know. My father's beard had long gone gray, and he also had a few silver strands in his hair, but according to my friends that just made him look hotter.

And every time they said that it made me want

to throw up even more than I nearly did while holding my nephew as he filled his diaper.

There were lines that you did not cross.

"Lief is far too delighted over his kid's diaper, and I don't even want to think about that," Colin said with a shudder.

"If you ever decide to become a father, you'll be proud too. And disgusted. And wanting to run away. But thankfully Leif has nerves made of steel," my mom teased.

"I like how Brooke and Dad are out with the other two kids and that leaves Leif alone with the baby. Meaning he came here so we could all help," Gideon said with a roll of his eyes.

My lips twitched. "I may not like changing diapers, but I love babies."

"Thinking of babies of your own?" Gideon teased, and I flipped him off, regardless that Mom watched us both.

"Stop teasing your sister, although, I haven't heard about any dates in a while, should I be worried?"

My cheeks heated as I blushed, and I glared at my twin. "I've been busy."

"I see," my mom said, and I was afraid she probably did.

It wasn't that I didn't want to date. It was that I couldn't find the right person. I had an amazing family, fantastic brothers, and the best father in the world. That was a lot to live up to. Plus every time I went on a date, I swear a Montgomery popped out of nowhere, saying they were just milling about, waiting to descend on us and embarrass me. They might not try to, but it just happened. Naturally.

"You have had a few projects come up all at once, it makes sense that you've been busy," Colin said, saving me. Although Gideon and I were twins and therefore always close, Colin and I were the closest in terms of our personalities, and how he took care of me.

I was the first person he came out to, although the rest of our family had already known. He had been safe with us, and of course that meant my mother had tried to set him up with men and women, because Mom wanted all of us to find love. While Colin was divorced, and Gideon was still figuring out if he could date everybody in his sphere, I was on a dating moratorium.

I had to be.

Nobody seemed to be able to push *him* out of my mind. Not that I was going to be thinking about Sharp. And as if my phone knew what I was thinking, it buzzed in my pocket. A buzz I'd been waiting for since it had been nearly twenty-four hours since the last text. It could have been anyone else, but I *knew* it was him.

The others were talking, and I tried to pull up my phone nonchalantly so they wouldn't notice.

Sharp: Are you ready for the visit to the small town of small towns next week? Don't forget your boots.

"Who's that?" Gideon asked, as he reached from my phone.

I snapped it back from him and growled. "Hey. Hands off."

"What? I'm just curious."

"You're being nosy," my mom said, as she squeezed my shoulder. "I'm sure if it was something important, she would let us know. Like perhaps a certain *somebody*?" she asked, drawing out the word.

I pressed my lips together and slipped my phone back into my pocket. I would answer later, maybe.

It wasn't like Sharp and I were anything. We were just friends. He'd literally been engaged and awkwardly left at the altar. He and I texted because we were friends, and we had met in a dramatic set of circumstances, but it wasn't like I wanted him. Or was ever going to be with him. I lived in Denver. He lived in Clover Lake. When my cousin Livvy had fallen for Ewan, they had tried to make long distance work, and it had nearly broken them. So, Livvy had ended up moving to Clover Lake with her daughter, working from there, and starting over. And while us Montgomerys visited Clover Lake often, she was all alone up there.

I liked being near my family, however claustrophobic it may be at times. I wasn't someone who changed my life for a man, a man who was in love with his ex. Because he had to be. Not that he'd ever told me that when we had the opportunity. There was no way you could just put in a text that you were broken and in love and feeling poorly.

Instead, we just talked about our days. Like how he worked at the ranch, and the name of his horse. He would send me photos of my niece Amelia. Technically Amelia wasn't my niece because Livvy and I were cousins, but when it came to our generation, we had decided everybody's kids were our nieces and nephews. To figure out family trees made our brains hurt and we gave up.

Either way however, there was nothing between me and Sharp. Just a few texts. Every day.

And the fact that I was going to visit Clover Lake again as I could do my job from anywhere in the world usually. And Livvy did need family around her. Family that wasn't just the McBrides.

At least this trip had to go better than the first trip that had been cut too short.

"Anyway, are you ready for your trip to Clover Lake? I know you've been busy trying to make sure that you have everything set up at Montgomery Inc. I just hope you're not putting too much on your shoulders."

I relaxed at that, ignoring my brothers' looks. They were far too curious for their own good, even with our age gaps.

Of course that just reminded me that Sharp and I had around a ten-year age gap. Not that it was a thing. It couldn't be a thing because he and I were just friends. We texted. And I was going to see him in a week.

I needed to stop thinking about him. "I'm excited to see Livvy and Amelia. I hate that they live so far away, but the McBride Ranch is beautiful."

"We still need to get out there," my mother said as she moved us towards the dining room where we had lunch set up. "It's been two months since your father and I went on a vacation."

"Didn't you and Dad just go on a motorcycle

ride up to Estes Park? That counts as a vacation," Gideon said as he took a seat across from me.

"If you think that's a vacation, no wonder you're perpetually single," Colin mocked as he began plating up everybody's sandwiches.

Although my mother had set everything up, Leif and I had made the sandwiches, and Colin and Gideon would clean up. We each had a set goal when it came to sharing chores, even though none of us lived here any longer.

I liked being able to come back home whenever I wanted, and I lived close enough to make that happen.

I worked for the family, though I had known that's what I was going to do when I got out of college. There were many businesses with my family, but I worked at one of the originals, the main construction company that my aunts and uncles had formed along with my grandfather. It had taken different incarnations over the years, but now I worked directly with my Aunt Tabby as well as on my own with Montgomery Builders—the next generation version of the company. Aunt Tabby was the head admin for their company and all the subsidiary companies that came from Montgomery Inc. She could run everything with just her pinky and that planner of hers. I had loved following Aunt Tabby around with my own little binder and stickers, making little notes in my planner. My mother had just rolled her eyes and made sure I got a new yearly planner for school, and for life. Then she would make sure that they were color coded, so I would know which is which.

I was still like that even though the majority of my life was online. I loved the tactile feeling of paper and organizing. I was one of the head admins for the company, and while my aunt worked with people face-to-face, as did most of my family, I did everything behind the scenes. Meaning I worked from home most days. And when I visited Clover Lake or traveled with my siblings or friends, I was still able to work. I was grateful that I was able to do that. It gave me options that not everybody else had.

"So, what did I miss?" Leif asked as he walked in, Beau settled in his arms, in a new onesie and smelling all clean and like a baby.

"I want to know who Jamie is texting," Gideon blurted.

Colin then threw me under the bus. "And why she's all of a sudden so excited to visit Clover Lake."

I glared but resisted the urge to flip them off.

Not that my mother would care, as I had already done that in front of her once today, but no, because I wouldn't flip off family in front of the baby. I had standards.

So I mouthed the words *fuck you* to both, making sure Beau couldn't see, and promptly took a bite of my sandwich.

Leif whistled through his teeth, before my mother plucked the baby from his arms, and he sat down to lunch. This was my family, what I loved. And what I strived for. No matter how much I wanted to return that text, and visit Clover Lake next week, coming home to this was what mattered.

And I knew that was never going to change.

———

"You're here!" Livvy said as she threw her arms around me. I'd barely been able to get out of my SUV—the same one that a wet and grumpy Sharp had gotten into—before she'd nearly knocked me down.

"I'm glad to be here too. I love you bunches."

Livvy danced on her toes as she looked me over, that bright light of her eyes bringing me so much joy. She deserved this happiness. "I hope you packed enough to stay a whole month."

I rolled my eyes. "I did. And I think you have this thing called a washer and dryer? Or are we so set in the frontier days of Wyoming that I'm going to have to use a bucket and beat my clothes with some rocks."

"I see you're making fun of Wyoming again," Ewan said as he strolled forward, wearing his work jeans, boots, and a backwards baseball cap. Though to be honest, I'd been expecting a cowboy hat.

While a few people in Colorado wore them, I didn't really head to the rural areas to see that happen. I'd been to a couple of bars where tourists wore them, but unless I went to a place like the Grizzly Rose to line dance, they weren't the norm. The fact that the McBrides sometimes wore them for work and celebrations, and had different hats for each, always amused me.

They were real ranchers of Angus beef. Well, I thought it was Angus. Or maybe that was just Angus McBride, the patriarch of the family. I needed to learn more about how this ranch operated because this was Livvy's family.

Nothing else.

My gaze slid over the crew as they welcomed

me, and I hugged Becky McBride, Ewan's mother, as well as Angus, and tried to spot the one face I was looking for. The one face I knew I shouldn't.

Gwendolyn McBride, Ewan's younger sister, ran forward and hugged me tightly. "I'm so glad that you're here. We need more estrogen around this place."

"Hey, there's nothing wrong with testosterone," Galen said as he puffed out his chest. He looked like a blend of Ewan and Sharp, and it just reminded me that genetics were funny that way.

"Excuse me, are you really going to be the one discussing testosterone with me?" Ewan said dryly, as Galen moved forward and put his sister in a headlock.

"Kids. Seriously? We have company."

I waved them off and hugged Becky harder. "It's okay. I have three older brothers. I'm used to it."

"And this is why I'm glad I just have the one younger brother," Livvy said dryly, as she rolled her eyes. I said hello to a few other McBrides, apparently the cousins who worked on the ranch or nearby, and a few ranch hands, before finally coming back and hugging Amelia as she wrapped her arms around my waist. I kissed the top of her head, realizing she was getting taller by the day, and held her close.

However, there was only one person I didn't see.

I swallowed hard, trying to hide my disappointment.

He knew I was on my way. I'd texted him after all. It wasn't like we had plans to see each other. It was probably better that we just texted anyway.

Livvy met my gaze and raised a single brow. Apparently, my look of disappointment hadn't gone unnoticed. Not that it mattered. It was just a look. That's what I told myself at least.

"Anyway, we're going to set you up in the guest cabin. I know you stayed at our house last time, but since you're going to be here a whole month to work, and to spend time with us, I figured you'd like your own space."

I beamed at that. "Really? A cabin on a ranch? I don't know if I brought the right stickers for my planner."

"I have stickers for you, Aunt Jamie," Amelia said as we swung our arms together, walking towards the cabin.

"Those are the words to a girl's heart," I teased.

"She has her own little planner," Ewan said dryly before they brought up something about the ranch I didn't understand. I smiled, listening as they spoke of their plans for the workday, and what needed to happen on the ranch.

While Clover Lake was a small town, one right outside of Sheridan, about five hours or so from Fort Collins, the Cabell Ranch pretty much engulfed the west side of it. The McBride Ranch covered I think 1,400 acres last time they mentioned it, and they raised Angus and a few other things, their neighbors raised Hedford. I had to look up what each of those were. They also had sheep for wool, and they set aside acres that they rotated for hay. They had a few horses, and I knew that Sharp wanted to bring in more because he had texted me about it. They weren't a horse ranch, or whatever that was called, but he had a few that he used for breeding and wanted to add more to the business. From what the text said, Angus McBride was excited about it, though I didn't know if they had talked about it more.

Not that it was my business.

The cabin was close by, on the east side of Ewan and Livvy's home, but as I looked around, I realized there was another home a little bit closer.

"That is Sharp's house," Ewan said, and I determinedly didn't look at Livvy.

"If you need anything, and the phone's out or something, you just head over to Sharp. He knows what he's doing."

"Oh. Really?" Well, my voice had definitely squeaked just then, and not only had Livvy noticed, but Ewan did too. "So what are you guys doing today? Anything I can help with?"

"Are you going to become a ranch hand?" Ewan asked, teasing.

"You want me nowhere near anything that I could break. There's a reason that I'm an admin with the construction crew."

"Good to know. Well come on, I'll show you what we've been working on, especially with the expansion, after we drop everything in the cabin."

"That sounds great. I've been sitting for so long, I could use the walk."

"You'll be walking around here a lot," Livvy said, as she hugged me again. "I'm truly so glad that you're here. The fact that you can take a whole month to work while you're visiting just means the world to me."

I kissed my cousin's cheek and held on tight.

"Of course. We miss you down there, but I know we all visit enough that it has to be annoying at times."

"Never," Livvy and Ewan said at the same time, and as Livvy let go of me, she met her husband's gaze, and the love I saw there nearly staggered me.

I swallowed hard and made my way through the home. The place was gorgeous with its tall ceilings and arched doorways. There were multiple open areas so the family could gather, but also closed off areas so the noise wouldn't overwhelm quiet sections. It was absolutely brilliant and stunning. I wasn't jealous of my cousin. Not really. But I loved that kind of love, and I didn't even know what it felt like. I pushed those thoughts to the side as they had no place here and followed the small family as they made their way towards the main ranch. We had to get in a golf cart of all things, because it was such a large spread, but I didn't mind. Amelia was buckled next to me, talking a mile a minute, and I settled in, knowing that while I had to work, it would be good to relax.

"We're setting up an expansion for more horses. It's Sharp's baby, and he's been focusing on that. That's why he didn't stop by to say hello and greet you," Ewan said, as he took Livvy's hand and moved her towards the edge of the paddock. At least I thought it was a paddock. I truly needed to look up the names of these things. I smiled as I watched different horses moving in different sections. I wanted to bring out my planner notebook and take down notes. I liked learning things, and it was the part of me that always made my mom smile.

Ewan explained a few more things, and I listened with half an ear, as I leaned against the metal grate, smiling as everything settled in. This was Livvy's home, and it was gorgeous. It wasn't Denver, it wasn't family, and yet, it called to me. Or maybe I was just too tired.

When I looked up, the hairs on the back of my neck stood on end, and I realized that there was somebody coming towards us.

I swallowed hard as Sharp moved forward, his hat shielding his eyes from the sun, his thick thighs covered in dirt, his boots even more marred in clay. But he had a grin on his face, as he called out something I couldn't quite hear.

My heart raced, and I nearly kicked myself. What the hell was wrong with me?

This was Sharp. Just a friend who I texted. I was not here for him. Not only was he probably still in love with Jo, he was my cousin's brother-in-law. That made him off limits.

But then his gaze met mine, and I blinked, feeling as if someone punched me in the chest. I staggered back, my shoulder hitting the metal pin holding the gate closed.

Sharp's eyes widened, as he began to pick up his pace, and then everything moved slowly. The gate behind me swung open, and I fell, hands outstretched, as my back hit the packed dirt.

My elbow hit the ground hard, and stars buzzed in front of my eyes, as the sound of hooves hitting soil hammered behind me.

And then somebody screamed.

CHAPTER THREE

Sharp

As soon as Jamie's feet ended up over her head, my speed picked up even more, and I practically ran towards the paddock. Out of the corner of my eye, I saw Ewan running as well, since Lightning had also noticed Jamie's fall.

I cursed under my breath, because I hated that gate. We had been reusing an older section to get the layout, and now that single mistake was going to end up getting Jamie hurt.

Ewan jumped over the fence as I went through

the gate, and both of us threw up our hands, trying to calm Lightning down.

However, Lightning had a particular temper. He did not like surprises, most people, kids, or rainy days. Though he did love Amelia. We weren't sure why, maybe she gave him sugar cubes when we weren't looking, but Lightning had an attitude.

He was also a damn good horse who was learning the idea of calm.

I'd just wish he'd learn it a bit quicker.

"Whoa," I said, as I slowly made my way to the right side of the encircled area where Jamie was just now rolling to her knees. "Jamie, I want you to stay still for a moment."

Lightning began to pace back and forth, letting out little huffs and chuffs, and I winced.

"Oh dear."

My lips nearly twitched at the sound of her voice, but she was awake, and that meant she'd be able to move quickly when needed.

Lightning moved a little bit closer, stomping at the ground, before Ewan was there, rope in hand, and I moved quickly.

In an instant, Lightning noticed our movements and shifted towards us, but then my hands were on Jamie's hips, and I lifted, took four steps back, and let Galen—who had shown up right when I'd made it to Jamie—shut the gate behind us. Ewan had already jumped out of the paddock on the other side, and Lightning paced between us, looking annoyed that he hadn't gotten to trample anyone.

"Well that was embarrassing," Jamie said against my chest, and that's when I realized I was still holding her, one hand on her hip, the other on the back of her head, keeping her close.

I wasn't sure why I liked that feeling so much, and I would think about that later. Maybe. Or I wouldn't think about it at all. After all I had known Jamie would be visiting soon and so far I had spent more time here in the horse area rather than welcoming her.

It had been six months since the disaster that was my lack of wedding, and while my family had given up razzing me about it because there was no point when we knew it hadn't been my fault, our town hadn't been so easy.

Clover Lake was a decently sized town in Wyoming, for what it's worth. However, it was still one of those small towns that continued to have gossip like nobody's business. There was at least one of everything—a mercantile store, a diner, a coffee shop, a bakery, a lumber store, a ranching store, and a supply and repair store that I refused to go into.

And with all of that came people who loved to judge. The McBrides, as well as our neighbors who Ewan had been friends with for years, were the outliers when it came to Clover Lake. We were the ones with larger pieces of land and brought in the taxes and income streams that helped feed a lot of the town. Hence, the resentment from those who either used to work with us or never wanted to. We weren't the town settlers of Clover Lake, nor were we the founders. We were just a family who worked here. And any time you could kick a McBride down, most of Clover Lake loved it.

That's why I was still the talk of the town, but I wasn't alone.

No, there was also Jamie.

A woman that I shouldn't be thinking of. A woman that I had been texting daily for the past six months, if not more. And a woman that I was still holding on to. With a sigh, I let her go, staggering back slightly.

I immediately pulled my hat off and flipped it backwards so I could see her better.

"Are you okay? Are you hurt? We need to replace that gate. When we set up this section, we used an older piece of equipment just to sketch it out, but we need to fix that."

I reached out and tucked a piece of that hot pink hair behind her ear, and froze, realizing that I was once again touching her. I needed to stop doing that.

Jamie blinked at me, her cheeks going red. "I'm really okay. I sort of hit my arm, but not really. Because I'm a dork. I'm so sorry if I got anybody in trouble, or if I ruined something or if someone was hurt."

I barely resisted the urge to run my hands down her arms to check her out and keep her safe. What was it about this woman? "You didn't do anything wrong. I promise you. I'm sorry that you even ended up in that position though."

"I can't believe I just fell into a horse thingy."

My lips twitched. "Horse thingy?"

"You're the rancher. I don't know these words."

"Well, I'm glad that you're okay."

"All is well." She looked down at her elbow and frowned. "Except for this minor cut here."

I moved forward quickly, taking her arm. "Fuck. Come on, I can go get you a bandage or call the doctor or something."

Seriously? It was a tiny cut. What the hell was wrong with me? It had to be the same thing that had pushed me into texting her *daily* all of these months. I needed a reality check.

And thankfully that reality check came in the form of my brother, as Ewan and Galen both came forward.

"That's one way to start the day," Galen said as he moved forward, taking Jamie in his arms.

I narrowed my gaze at him, muttering under my breath. Galen just winked and hugged her tightly. When she wrapped her arms around him for a hug, I wasn't jealous at all. I shouldn't be jealous.

"I'm an idiot. But I'm okay. I'm so glad that everybody was here to watch that happen though."

"We wouldn't be the McBrides without watching family members fall into things. You should have seen the time that Sharp fell into the creek and ended up cutting his—"

"We're not going to tell that story," I cut him off.

"Wait. Well now I need to know."

"You really should. Don't worry, we'll talk about it over dinner. You are coming for dinner tonight, right? All of us McBrides are there since Gwen is back in town."

"I'm so glad that she was able to be here during my month-long visit. You guys are going to be so tired of me by the end of this trip."

"Not a chance," I blurted, and Galen gave me a knowing look as Jamie's cheeks pinked.

"I am glad that you're okay," Ewan put in as Livvy came forward and pulled Jamie to her side.

"I can't take you anywhere, cousin of mine. You really are a suburban girl through and through."

"Tell me about it," Jamie said as she pushed her bangs from her eyes.

My hand had wanted to reach out and push those bangs just like before. And I needed to stop that. I froze, realizing I shouldn't have touched her. And definitely not when the rest of the family had been looking.

"Anyway, I'm sorry that I made a spectacle of myself. I will go with Livvy now and figure out where to sit at my office since I will be working."

"You didn't make a spectacle of yourself, Jamie. We're just glad that you're okay." I ignored the knowing looks from my brothers.

"Well, okay. I'm going to go now. And maybe put ice on something."

Her eyes danced, and I couldn't help but notice the heat. What the hell was wrong with me?

I did not have this reaction around women. Yes, I liked them, but even before I had started dating Jo, I'd been hands off. I didn't go out with different women often, and I was probably the most celibate of my entire family. Ewan hadn't dated often, and Gwen and Galen didn't go out that much. I tended to stay home. Or if I was out with friends, I didn't go home with random women. I didn't have this need or desire when it came to other people in my life.

And yet from the moment I had seen Jamie—even when I shouldn't have—I had wanted to be next to her. I had felt that heat, that connection. And from the look in her eyes, I swore she felt it too. Or maybe I was just hoping for more than what was there.

Livvy pulled her away, going over any injuries again, and I ignored both Ewan and Galen's pointed looks.

"I'm going to go check on Lightning."

"The team's working on him. He's just fine. Are you planning on telling me what the hell that was about?" Ewan asked, his voice careful.

"I have no idea what you're talking about."

"Well, that's a lie. You couldn't keep your hands off little Ms. Montgomery," Galen said softly, though his voice wasn't that low.

"That's not it, and I would take kindly for you not to say shit like that with people around. You know how this town is." I paused. "And you know how this town feels about Jamie."

Galen winced as Ewan cursed.

"Has Livvy told her about what's going on?" I asked softly.

"I don't think so. How do you bring up the concept of small-town drama to someone who doesn't live it? It's not as bad as it could be, but people in Jo's corner are weird."

"Jo needs to step back," Galen snarled. "Her whole family does. Her brothers are a bunch of nits, and her father needs to be taken down a peg."

"Tell me how you really feel," I said dryly, even as a twinge of guilt seeped in. I had brought this on all of us by accepting Jo's proposal. Because she had been the one to propose. Which had been sort of accidental, and we'd ended up going along with the wedding despite the fact that neither one of us really loved each other.

And in the end, she hadn't been able to find a way out of it without making me a spectacle, and therefore Jamie one.

I would never forgive her for that, and yet, the blame wasn't solely on her shoulders. I could have walked away long before that. And it didn't matter how many times I told the town and the little busybodies out there that I hadn't cheated, and Jamie had nothing to do with it, there were a few who loved painting her with the scarlet A.

"You're going to talk to her about it?" Galen asked, meeting my gaze.

"Since she'll be here for a month and probably wants to go to the few streets Clover Lake calls downtown, I should. Or Livvy should."

"She'll probably mention it," Ewan answered to the unasked question.

"But you should talk to her. Considering you two seem to be the center of all of this. Even though you don't know each other."

I looked down at the ground for a moment, and Ewan cursed under his breath. "It's not true, is it?"

My gaze shot up, my fist tightening. "Are you fucking kidding me right now? No. I'm not a cheater. I literally met Jamie for the first time when she picked me up on the side of the road. Because that asshole William kidnapped me."

"I'm sorry for asking." Ewan rubbed the back of his neck. "Seriously. I don't actually believe you're a cheater. Fuck. I'm sorry."

"Why didn't you ever press charges?" Galen asked, his voice low. "He could have killed you."

That thought had occurred to me more than

once. In the months since the incident as we all called it, my family had rallied around me when they realized that I had been drugged, kidnapped, and left on the side of the road where anybody could have attacked me. We all knew it had to be William. But we had no proof. William was the one who knew how to do shit like that and had been known to hogtie people in high school, then toss them in the back of a truck and pretend it had something to do with a prank. More than once me or my brothers, and even Gwendolyn once, had saved some poor kid from being left out in a field by William and his friends.

"William might not have a badge anymore, but he still has friends at the department. I have zero proof, just a hunch."

"We see the way that those two act around you. And how both of their families like to perpetuate the idea that it was your fault."

"And that's not proof."

"The fact that Jo and William are already married infuriates me," Ewan snarled.

"Other than they keep bringing up the incident, and possibly harming Jamie's reputation? Don't fucking care anymore. They are welcome to have each other."

"Well good. Although at some point you might want to tell us exactly why you decided to marry her," Galen said snidely.

"I think that answer's I have no idea why. Now let's get back to work, because the crew is standing around and staring at us, and I'm already the talk of this town."

"It's just going to get worse when Jamie walks through it. You know that. You should warn her."

I ran my hand over my face and slid my hat forward. "On it."

I moved past my brothers, nodded at a few of our team, who we all trusted, but I didn't know what they thought when they saw me. Did they see a cheater? The one who left Jo at the altar?

Because in the end, we had left each other. Or rather, I had been pushed.

But nobody would believe me. Not even when they knew the farm truck had been put on the side of the road with no keys. I was the one who was blamed, because I was the one who didn't spread lies and shit.

I moved past the barn, and stepped towards my truck, only to stop short when a familiar blonde with pink streaks stood next to it, her teeth worrying into her lip.

"Jamie? Is something wrong?"

I was moving so quickly, that I didn't even realize that I was near her until I could feel the heat of her next to me.

"No. I just wanted to say hi. Livvy had a phone call, and I decided to walk towards your truck. It looks great. I mean, not that I got to see it before."

My lips twitched, and I slipped my hands into my pockets, unsure of myself for the first time in a long while. "Yeah, I like it. It's not exactly new, but it gets the job done. Better than the farm truck that you passed."

"I would never say that."

"Your SUV is pretty nice though. Thanks for letting me borrow it."

Jamie threw her head back and laughed. "When I told my parents that story, they still couldn't quite believe that I had just given my keys to some stranger. Yes, your brother might be married to my cousin, but you were still a stranger."

"Hey, are we really strangers when you meet me on the side of the road and pick me up like a hitchhiker?"

"Again, my dad wasn't too pleased with that. Or any of my three brothers."

I winced. "I've met two of your brothers before,

and they seem like nice guys. They won't beat me up, right?"

"I can't tell you that." She practically sing-songed it, and I snorted.

"Well, my brothers won't beat you up. Gwen though?"

"Well, she could take me no matter what. I may work in construction, but I'm still pretty dainty." She flexed her muscles, and I barely resisted the urge to reach out to caress her arm.

I was losing my damn mind.

"Anyway, I just wanted to say hi." She looked down at her shoes, and I let out a breath.

"Hi, Jamie. It's good to see you even though we text often enough."

She looked up at me then, a smile on her face. "Yeah. I'm glad that I was able to steal your number from Livvy's phone to check in. It's been nice chatting with you."

"Same. I feel like we know each other already, which is weird, right?"

"So weird." She let out a relieved breath. "I have no idea what I'm doing here, Sharp. I realize that I'm here for Livvy, and Amelia, and I enjoy spending time with my cousin, but I was happy to see you too. Which I cannot believe I'm even saying this aloud. I do not talk about my feelings like this."

"When you said that you were coming to stay for a month, I had no idea what I was supposed to do with myself," I said honestly.

Her eyes widened. "Sharp."

"I'm not in love with her. I don't think I ever was." I frowned at that. "Which isn't the greatest thing for me to say. But I don't know, all these months texting? I'm just glad that you're here."

"I have to go back home after a month though," she whispered, saying the words that I knew were true, and that couldn't help but bring reality into this awkward yet new situation that we found ourselves in.

"A month." I let out a breath. "I could work with a month."

"And what does that mean?" she asked, her gaze not meeting mine.

I leaned down and pressed my lips against hers. I didn't mean to do it. It was stupid beyond all reason. She was Livvy's cousin, didn't live here, and there was no lead-up to this. And yet I couldn't help but think about the dreams that I had had of her. The need to touch her since I had first laid eyes on her. The connection I couldn't quite grasp.

And when she parted her mouth, I slid my tongue against hers and moaned. I cupped her face, deepening the kiss as her hands went to my chest, her fingers tightening ever so slightly. And when I pulled back, I pressed my forehead to hers.

"That's probably a complication."

"There's no probably about that. Because now I have to go to family dinner with you and pretend I didn't just let you kiss me."

"You kissed me back," I teased.

"Yes. I did. And well, I guess we'll figure out what that means later."

I tucked her hair behind her ear and smiled. "I'd say we will figure it out, but we both know I'm pretty bad at that."

She laughed. "I'll see you around, Sharp McBride. Thank you for the kiss."

And with that, she walked away, looking far more confident than I felt.

I put my hands over my face and resisted the urge to growl. Just with one kiss, I was lost. There was something seriously wrong with me. I had never felt like this before, because it wasn't love at first sight. I didn't love her. I didn't even know her beyond the secrets that we had told each other over the past six months.

But it was a connection at first sight, and that scared me more than anything.

Because she was right, we didn't live near, we had lives far separate from each other, and Clover Lake was already out to get her.

And once I figured out a way to tell her, she was never going to forgive me.

Chapter Four

Jamie

"When you said small town, I sort of forgot what small town meant." I stared out the window, eyes wide as we drove into the town that was Clover Lake.

I had lived in Denver and its surrounding suburbs my entire life. My dad's tattoo shop was in downtown Denver, with my mom's boutique right across the street. In fact, that was how they met. Their love story was one of the more romantic tales I had ever heard, and part of the reason why I was careful with who I dated. They knew love, and it had no bounds when it came to them. They understood each other, cared for each other, and were just good for one another. I wanted someone like that in my life, even though I had no idea where that would come from.

And because I loved my parents and enjoyed being with them, I had gone to college in Colorado and worked for the family business. It didn't matter that I could do my job in any state or practically country, I enjoyed being near my family.

So as a suburban and city girl through and through, Clover Lake was a complete oddity to me.

"Keep your mouth closed, or you're going to catch flies."

"Are you learning different colloquialisms now?" I asked, holding back a laugh.

"Maybe. I keep adding little ranch hand jokes to my repertoire and scaring my father."

"I love Uncle Shep."

"My dad is pretty cool. And he's enjoying visiting his granddaughter in Wyoming. Just like I'm so excited that you are here for a whole month. You are going to get tired of me and Clover Lake."

I looked at Livvy then, and how happy she was. I missed seeing Livvy every week. It wasn't that I saw and hung out with all of my cousins weekly or even monthly. There were enough of us spread out that sometimes we only saw each other in passing, but there were the group texts that Livvy was still part of. However, Livvy living in Wyoming was possibly the best thing for her.

And it was because of Ewan and the McBrides. Amelia was already calling Ewan daddy, and the three of them were a unit. A family.

And her in-laws had already adopted Livvy into the folds and didn't mind housing any Montgomery that came to visit. Honestly at some point visiting Livvy would just be an excuse to see the beauty that was this small town.

Clover Lake was situated on the outskirts of an actual lake. There were multiple streets, but the main street—actually called Main Street—housed many of the businesses that brought in locals and out-of-towners.

"At some point we'll take you to the diner for dinner and I know it doesn't sound that interesting, but it has amazing food."

"Sharp mentioned that the chicken fried steak was fantastic. The gravy especially."

As Livvy parked in front of a small coffee shop, she turned and gave me a look before she clicked off the engine. "Sharp did, did he? When were you going to tell me that you were texting my brother-in-law as much as you were? Because while I know you stole his phone number to apparently say you were sorry for the whole wedding fiasco that you had nothing to do with, you didn't mention you kept speaking with him."

Blushing, I ignored my cousin and turned around to wave at Amelia who was in her booster.

"Are you ready to show me around Clover Lake?"

"Yes! And see Uncle Sharp." She fluttered her eyelashes, and I blushed, wondering when the sarcasm gene settled in for the Montgomerys. Perhaps at birth.

"Okay, time for some fresh air."

"Before you get out, I need to tell you something that I should have told you weeks ago, or perhaps Sharp should have told you."

I froze, tension suddenly seizing me. "What is it?"

I looked through the front windshield and blinked as a woman with dark hair, and a beautiful sun dress, glared at me. She smiled at Livvy, and kept moving, and my cousin cursed under her breath.

"What was that about?" I asked, my voice going slightly high-pitched.

"Well, apparently. Um."

"You're not helping this situation," I said softly, wondering what I had done wrong. Of course, there was only one thing that I could have technically done wrong when it came to this town, but surely it wasn't that.

"The town is very sweet. And loving. But there's a few people who are a little judgmental. In the way that people are."

"Livvy, just spit it out already."

Livvy looked at the rearview mirror and I knew she was checking on Amelia, and I let out a breath.

"Jo and her family enjoy stirring up gossip. They always have. Which was one reason why I didn't know why she was with Sharp to begin with, but I digress."

I let that little bit of envy that Jo and Sharp had been together at all wash away because it had nothing to do with me. I had merely kissed Sharp—which was a horrible mistake most likely—and it didn't mean that I had any possession over him.

"Okay. But isn't Jo married to William?"

Livvy's eyes widened. "Sharp told you that? Oh good. Though I still have so many questions."

"He mentioned that she got married, and we talked about it. Because I know that he's over her."

Livvy winced. "He is. I know he is. I don't know when he was together with her in the way that getting married made sense, but that doesn't make any sense right now. Anyway, Jo and her mother, her brothers, and some of the townsfolk who love gossip, are deciding that you are a..."

Her voice trailed off, and I glared. "I'm a what?"

"A homewrecker."

"Homewrecker!" Amelia called out, and I closed my eyes and counted to five. I could not make it to ten. "I'm about to say words that are bad for Amelia, so maybe we should take a walk."

"The McBrides and everyone else are quickly dispelling the rumors. It's stupid. They're stupid. And I know we don't call people stupid, right Amelia?"

"Right."

"But I thought maybe you should know before we walk around in Clover Lake."

"Maybe you should have told me this before I decided to spend a month in a small town that apparently doesn't want me here."

Before Livvy could say anything to that, I hopped out of the SUV, rolled my shoulders back, and glared at a woman who had wrinkled her nose when she looked at me.

Oh good. Glaring at strangers was going to do wonders for me trying to settle in and show that I wasn't a homewrecker or a terrible person. Brilliant job, Jamie Montgomery.

"I'm sorry. I know we should have told you this," Livvy said, as she came around the car with Amelia in tow. "You did not do anything wrong," she added, her voice low.

There were a few people out and about, but nobody was paying attention to us at this point. I guess I could count that as a win for now. However, I was still more than confused.

"Should I go?" I asked, suddenly feeling far more unwanted than I'd ever had in my life. In fact, I wasn't sure when I had ever felt like this. Perhaps when I had tried out for the cheerleading team and had gotten runner up to the alternate. All because I wouldn't sleep with the lacrosse team captain. He had told his best friend to tell his girlfriend who happened to be the cheerleading captain, that I was a terrible person, and added a few choice words.

That unwelcome feeling had lasted for approximately two weeks until I had joined the swim team, and had been immediately enveloped by happy people. Then I had done volleyball, and might've accidentally, most likely on purpose, nearly broken the cheer captain's nose during a layup. But it really wasn't my fault.

Either way, I'd always been liked. Loved. And I'd never even been dumped before.

Maybe I was a little sheltered because I'd had a good childhood, a good life, and people that I cared about and who cared about me in turn, but that didn't make this whole thing any sense normal or as if I earned it.

"Hey there, Livvy," a woman with auburn hair said as she came forward, pushing her stroller. "It's so good to see you in town. I know you've been working hard. This must be your cousin Jamie, right? Gwen and Galen said that she would be in. Hi, I'm Amanda. It's lovely to meet you."

It was as if I had gone from a hot spring to a cold plunge and now sat in a sauna where I wasn't quite sure what the temperature was. This woman seemed so nice and genuinely looked happy to see me.

Did she not think I was a homewrecker?

Livvy moved forward and pulled Amelia in front of her. "It's good to see you, Amanda. And yes, this is Jamie. And she's in town for the whole month.

I'm trying to show her that the people of Clover Lake can be amazing."

Amanda winced and looked over her shoulder. "Ah. I see you've met some of the crew."

The way that she said the crew sounded as if it was in all caps, and a group that I wanted nothing to do with.

"I only mentioned it when Jo's aunt walked by," Livvy whispered.

"Apparently I'm a town pariah and nobody told me ahead of time."

Amanda gave Livvy a look and clucked her tongue. "No warning?"

"I thought it would be dissolved by now. It's been six months, and Jo's married."

"Let me get you guys a coffee, and we can sit down and catch up. And that way Amelia can stare longingly at her new boyfriend," Amanda said dryly, and I looked down to see Amelia and the boy in the stroller talking to each other using wild hand motions and looking absolutely smitten. There were a couple of years age difference for sure, and if anything, they looked as if they had secrets that nobody else could know, and I loved it so much. I wasn't surprised when Livvy immediately snapped a photo.

"I don't want to take up your day," I said, feeling slightly uneasy. Not because of Amanda, or even Livvy. But because I had no idea who was in that coffee shop, and if they hated me because they thought I was a homewrecker.

I don't think I'd ever said the word aloud before in my life, and I didn't want to start now.

"Let me welcome you to town and show you that there are good people here. The McBrides have been part of Clover Lake for generations, and my husband used to work with Sharp actually."

"Used to?" I asked, and Livvy gave me a look. And I knew that look. It was all because as soon as Sharp's name came up, I was like a prairie dog sticking their head out of the packed earth to see what was going on.

I was ridiculous, and I had no idea how I felt about Sharp. Not that I needed to feel anything about him at all.

He was just a guy I had picked up on the side of the road.

The one who made me catch my breath the moment I had seen him, even though it was exactly the wrong time.

The guy who I spoke to far too often. I had been lying to myself when I said once a week. It was once a day. Once a day we spoke. And now here I was, in a town that apparently hated me, at least part of its occupants did.

"He and his brothers went in on a piece of land outside of the McBrides'. I knew he was sorry to leave the ranch, but the McBrides help us out too." She went on to explain the type of ranch her family now owned, and I listened hard, trying to catch anything I could about regular operations. I never knew how much went into running a business like this and it was fascinating.

BECAUSE IT WAS NEW AND EXCITING.

Not that it had anything to do with Sharp.

I followed Livvy, Amanda, and the kids into the cute little coffee shop with bright pink and purple and Easter colored walls and smiled. It looked as if somebody had taken a watercolor painting and tossed it everywhere, so each thing was slightly unique, and soft and airy. Honestly, it looked more like a candy shop than a coffee shop, and when I saw the pastries, I realized, maybe that was for a reason.

"Oh, Livvy, Amanda, it's so good that you're here. Having a coffee fix is always the best way to go. And who's this?" an older woman asked as she set her glasses on top of her head.

I had a few family members who worked in the coffee industry or even had their own businesses. So I went into those places often enough that the people working there knew my name. But it wasn't that here. This woman would want to know who I was because I was with Livvy and Amanda. People that this woman knew.

I loved this small town feeling, as long as I ignored the odd look that a woman in a corner was giving me.

"This is my cousin, Jamie," Livvy said.

"Hi," I said, giving an awkward wave.

"Jamie, it's so good to see you. I am Clarissa, and I own The Roasted Bean. Not exactly the most unique name out there, but we love our coffee here. What can I get you?"

I looked through the menu, my mouth practically salivating at all the lovely options, and we each gave our orders. When I tried to slide my credit card in, Amanda was far too quick and waved us all off.

"This is my treat. You can get the next time."

The next time, because she assumed I would be around for it. I loved the idea, even though I was so confused. I had kissed Sharp and hadn't told Livvy. Oh, she probably had an idea something was going on, but she didn't know the thing that could change everything. Not that it should be that serious. I would walk away and nothing would happen.

The woman in the corner huffed as she grabbed her bags and stomped away, glaring at us, and Amanda surprised me by flipping her off, and Livvy just waved.

"Oh, I love you," Clarissa said as she set our coffees down. "That is Miss Hannah B. She enjoys gossip like no other and does everything that she can in life to be a complete pill. She's never been happy ever since she lost out on Miss Clover back in high school, and she hates the fact that it's been so many years since that high school debacle of hers."

I blinked, once again in awe of all the information these people had at their fingertips. Yes, you could say the Montgomerys were a small town of their own when it came to all of their intersecting lives, but it was nothing like this.

"Anyway, it's wonderful to have you here. And, if I hear anybody spreading any gossip that I don't like, they get kicked out. So if you want good caffeine in this town, you have to not be a dick." Clarissa winced. "Sorry about the language."

"She gets more than enough of that from her dad," Livvy said as she swept Amelia's hair back from her face.

My heart clutched at that sight, because Ewan was Amelia's dad. They were the cutest little family, and it wasn't that I was jealous, just confused as to what I wanted, and that was probably a problem.

I took a sip of my caramel latte with coconut chips and groaned. "This is stunning."

"Well, thank you. I'll be sure to get you addicted before you head out in a month. And next time if you come in alone, you can tell me all about your birth, your life, and all those gorgeous Montgomerys that I see coming in and out of here so often."

I threw my head back and laughed, grateful for this woman. I hadn't been able to visit the downtown last time. What with the whole runaway groom and canceled wedding, my trip had been cut short. But now I was being immersed in it—gossip and all—and I loved it.

"I'm sure I can bring up a few cousins next time," I added dryly.

"Don't. Clarissa will break all of their hearts, and then we'll have to deal with moping Montgomery men."

"The horror," Amanda teased.

We sat with our coffees, and I relaxed as they each told me a little bit more about town life, and I realized that Livvy was truly in her home and happy. This was the life that she had always wanted, as she had spent the first years of Amelia's life as a single mom.

Now things were different, and I was happy for her.

And she was probably never going to trust me again when she realized I kissed Sharp. And as if my thoughts had conjured him from thin air, a man with dark hair that I didn't recognize walked in with two McBrides right behind him.

When Amanda sighed at my side, I realized that that must be her husband. Livvy waved at Ewan, who came forward, picked Amelia up, then kissed his wife soundly on the mouth.

That left Sharp there, giving me an odd look, and I had no idea what to do with my hands.

"We were out and about and thought we'd kidnap you," Ewan said then he blew raspberries on Amelia's neck.

Those little girl giggles made me grin, and I just smiled.

"I'm kidnapping my wife and kid because we are

off to dinner. We'll see you this weekend?" Amanda's husband said before he turned to me. "I'm Jason, by the way. It's nice to meet you."

"It's nice to meet you too," I said. "I'm Jamie."

"Oh, I've heard all about you." He winked as he said it, and I turned to Sharp, who stared anywhere but me, but the tips of his ears were sure red.

Well, interesting.

"I'm kidnapping my wife, too," Ewan said, as he pulled Livvy to a standing position. "We have a date night." He turned to Sharp. "Do you mind taking Jamie home?"

I sputtered and gestured between all of them, wondering exactly who had thought of this plan. But when I glanced at Sharp, I realized that he looked just as confused as I did. Apparently, neither one of us had been hiding whatever connection we had been feeling very well.

Oops.

"I can do that," Sharp said softly, and between all of the goodbyes, the rustling of bags and people, I somehow found myself outside of the coffee shop standing in front of Sharp, wondering what the hell I was supposed to say.

Then I remembered the glaring women and knew exactly what I needed to say.

"Why didn't you tell me I was the town pariah?" I asked.

Sharp winced. "I'm the pariah. You are just—"

"The cheater. The home wrecker."

"But you're not. Everybody who knows us and actually likes us understands that. They'll get over whatever issues they're having later. I promise. Or I'll beat it out of Jo's brothers."

My lips twitched despite myself. "You did a fine enough job of it at the wedding."

"I could only beat up one brother. My cousin got the other. I'll have to change that next time."

He moved forward and brushed my hair back from my face. Anybody in town could be looking in that moment, but I didn't care. I was in so much trouble.

"Sharp," I began, my voice breathy.

"I know. Let me take you to dinner?" he asked.

We both paused, the unsaid words between us palpable. There could be no future in this. We both knew it.

"I'm a Montgomery."

"And I'm a McBride."

"And I live in Denver."

"And I live in Wyoming."

Our truths and lines in the sand. Everything that

told us that stepping any closer to the precipice of whatever this was would be a mistake. But instead he took my hand, squeezed, and led me towards the diner.

This was a mistake. I knew it. But it was one I was going to willingly make. A single dinner, a casual caress, that didn't mean a future, it didn't make a promise.

But I couldn't say no.

Chapter Five

Sharp

Two weeks later.

"YOU'RE TAKING THE ENTIRE AFTERNOON OFF? It's like I don't even know you." Galen lifted another box out of the truck and handed it to me. My muscles ached under the weight, but I ignored it. Just like I ignored my brother's teasing.

"Yes. An entire afternoon off. Something I know you enjoy doing. Often."

Galen rolled his eyes. "I'd flip you off, but my hands are already exhausted."

I smirked. "From having to jerk yourself off since you can't get a date?"

"Ha-ha," Galen said dryly. "You're so funny. I can't even."

"I'm just kidding. I'm sure you can get a date."

"Yes. I can. Much like you're dating a certain Montgomery."

I pressed my lips together, hoping that I didn't look too smug. Even though I was still fucking nervous. "We're not dating. We're just hanging out."

"She's only here for another couple of weeks, bruh."

"I realized that. It's why we're just hanging out."

"If you're sure. It worries me."

"Don't be worried. I'm just taking it easy. It's Jamie. I'm not going to hurt her." My voice was soft enough at the end of my words that my brother gave me a look.

"I know you don't want to hurt her, but it could still happen. And she could hurt you."

"*Galen.*"

"No. No. Go have fun, enjoy your afternoon off. And make sure that I take all the extra work for you."

"Yes, because I can see you're struggling here," I said dryly.

"I could be, you asshole."

"Language," Mom said as she came forward and kissed my cheek. "Get down off that truck, Galen. And come say hello to your mother."

"Didn't I say hello to you this morning?" Galen teased, before he leaped off the back of the truck and picked Mom up. He twirled her around, and she laughed as if she were a young girl, and I just rolled my eyes. My mother didn't have favorites. But sometimes I thought maybe Galen would be it. They just got along so well. Much like my sister and our father were practically best friends. Of course, I loved my parents, and we would do anything for each other, but my bond tended to be with Ewan. We all paired up nicely in this crazy family of ours.

"I'm headed to town. That damn town council meeting is going to be an entire afternoon event."

"Are you taking Dad with you?" I asked with a cringe.

"Yes. Because if I don't, who's going to hold me back from beating somebody up?" she asked.

"That's my mom, the one who's going to end up in jail for beating up a certain townie." Galen met my gaze, and I winced.

"We're not beating up that family." Again. I barely resisted the urge to smile at the memory of my mother putting my near-mother-in-law into a headlock.

Mom snorted. "No? They deserve it. You haven't heard the latest."

I winced. "What now?" My hands fisted at my sides.

"Nothing you need to worry about."

After a moment of silence, I leaned forward. "Mom."

"Seriously, everything's fine."

"You say that and yet I don't believe you."

"I'm just going to have to take that woman down a peg or two. The more she talks about my son and this family, the more she's going to regret it."

"As long as she doesn't hurt you." I sighed. "Hell, as long as she doesn't hurt any of our family. Even though we could take them."

"Damn straight. As is evidenced by the fact that they keep running their mouths because they know it's the only thing keeping them relevant. That woman is already married, and seemingly happy with that waste of space. I don't know why they feel it necessary to bring up old wounds."

I cursed under my breath, and once again

reminded myself that this was my fault. If I'd just done anything different and not been so selfish when it came to my relationships, we wouldn't have to deal with town council meetings and Jo's family. I knew they were still trying their best to create issues when it came to Jamie as well. It was frustrating when I couldn't protect her from the looks or the whispers. But she was holding her own every time she went to town. And like I had told Galen, she and I weren't dating. Because dating each other would be a mistake. We didn't live near each other, but we were spending time together. Every evening, and sometimes in the afternoons. But she worked and so did I. And her cabin was only a hundred feet from my house. Sometimes that hundred feet felt like a canyon. Sometimes it felt like it was next door. But a few kisses, a few caresses, didn't make a relationship. I knew that. And she knew that. And yet, it felt like if I didn't touch her soon, I would break. She was the only person I could think of, and she was constantly on my mind, and that was a fucking problem. Because she would go home soon, leaving me behind, like she should, and I wasn't sure what the hell I was supposed to do with that.

"Darling? What's wrong?"

I shook my head and pulled myself out of my dreary thoughts. "Nothing's wrong. Just thinking."

"About a certain date this afternoon?"

I glared at Galen, who held up his hands.

"Don't blame your brother. I saw your name on the list this afternoon for wanting time off, because we are a business and we know everything. And I know that you asked Franklin to get not only Giuseppe ready, but Rose as well," Mom said, speaking of my horse, and a gentle trail horse that I knew Jamie could handle. She wasn't comfortable in the saddle yet, and our ride this afternoon wasn't going to be long. But I would never put her on a horse that would hurt her.

"Oh, you're taking Rose out for her? Just make sure there's enough room on the door," Galen teased, and then ducked my fist.

"Boys. Stop fighting, especially when that joke wasn't even good," Mom deadpan.

"Hey. That's not nice. I'm your baby boy."

"And so is this baby boy. Now. Finish your chores and I'll go deal with Jo and her family of evil."

"Mom. You shouldn't have to."

"I was dealing with that woman's mother for

longer than you decided to stick your wick where you shouldn't have."

I sputtered, as Galen threw his head back and laughed. "Mom," I complained.

"What? It's the truth, isn't it? Now. I will continue to deal with that woman because we are a small town, and that is what we do. But she's a hazard. And she always has been. And she'll just have to learn not to mess the McBrides. She's jealous. She's jealous of our family, of our land, and of our place in this community. And she's nothing."

"I love you, Mom."

"I love you too. Now, go be a good son and take care of Jamie. She deserves a good afternoon."

"And by take care of, you mean?" Galen asked, before he ran away from our mother's glare.

"Why did you have to have another kid? I mean, Gwen's amazing. You could've skipped one."

"And not have my favorite? How dare you."

My mouth dropped as my mother just laughed, and she kissed me on the cheek. "Have fun. And remember, you're allowed to be happy, you know."

"Mom. We're just friends."

"Don't lie to me. I see the way that you look at each other."

"She doesn't live here, Mom. Being more than friends would be a mistake."

"Would it?" she asked, as she tilted her head, and then she left me alone, leaving me wondering what the hell I was going to do.

I finished setting up my project, knowing that I was lucky as hell to be a part of this family. We were a cow ranch, with a few other projects, but we didn't usually dabble in horses. But I wanted to add a breeding program. We had the space, and between my colleagues and myself, we had the expertise. We weren't going to be a large breeding program. Just large enough to ensure that we could get in the black soon, and provide a service for the town that we didn't have. Yes, Jo's family also bred horses, which was another point of contention, but we weren't going to be in the same realm. We wanted different things, which was always the problem when it came to me and Jo. I just hated the fact that my family had to deal with any of the consequences of my actions. I had been the one who had been cheated on, and yet some of the town still blamed me. However, that was what Jo wanted, and I was going to walk away from it. Because this afternoon was all about me and Jamie. And that brought a smile to my face.

With a sigh, I headed back to my house, jumped in the shower because I was covered in dust from work, though I knew I'd end up covered in more after the ride. But I wanted to smell nice for Jamie. Because we were friends. Who occasionally made out. And I was about to take her on a ride down one of my favorite trails.

This wasn't going to backfire at all.

I made it to the kitchens to pick up the picnic basket Cindy, our longtime cook, had prepped for me. She was the one had made sure that our family could stay alive during our childhood, since Mom and Dad had been working far too many hours to keep the ranch afloat. Then I headed to the barn for Giuseppe and Rose. Jamie was already there, talking with Franklin at the end of the stalls, and my heart kicked. This was going to be another problem. Because whenever I saw Jamie, everything froze.

She was a bright light. She made people smile and made them feel centered in her attentions. Every time I came up to her, when she was talking with someone else, she was always in the middle of helping them figure out something that they were having trouble with. Even if she didn't know all of the details behind ranching, if it had to do with organizing and planning, she was a queen. I knew she had already helped my mother with some planning when it came to an upcoming harvest and had even organized a spreadsheet for her. She fit in so well, and it scared me. Because in two weeks she would be gone, leaving me, us, behind.

She turned at the sound of my approach, a smile on her face so wide that I had to swallow hard.

When had someone ever looked at me like that before? It sure hadn't been Jo. No, I would stop comparing them. Because there was no comparison.

"Well, hello there," Franklin said with a grin.

I pulled my gaze from Franklin and swallowed hard as I stared at Jamie. My heart kicked a beat, annoying the fuck out of me because I was afraid my feelings were all over my face.

"Look at you with the cowgirl boots," I teased.

Jamie blushed and looked down at her boots. "They're technically Livvy's. We wear the same size shoe. I realize that they're formed to her feet. I'm probably going to ruin them, but I'll do my best not to."

"Girl needs herself a pair of boots," Franklin said, giving me another annoying look.

"We can make that happen," I said, my voice deep.

"Well, for when I visit," she said, bringing a

damper on my mood, but I pushed that aside. I wasn't going to think about that right now.

"Thanks for getting Rose and Giuseppe ready," I said to Franklin, and he just nodded.

"No problem. And thank Ms. Jamie here for helping me with my accounting spreadsheet. I thought I had it down, but she really knew how to organize it for me."

My brows rose as I looked over at her. "Really?"

"It only took a few minutes. I like organizing. I'm like my Aunt Tabby that way."

"She's a genius, don't let her tell you anything different."

"Oh, I know she's brilliant."

"And now that I'm blushing enough that I can feel heat radiating from my skin, let's go out for this ride. I'm going to end up walking bow-legged after, but I'm getting better at riding a horse."

"You're doing okay," I said dryly.

She rolled her eyes as I pulled out both horses, thanking Franklin in the end.

"So where are we off to?" she asked as I settled our lunch and the rest of our supplies in my saddlebags. We wouldn't be gone that long, but it was always good to keep some things in place in case of emergency.

"There's a creek that goes off the lake on the north side, and it has a pretty view. I like to go out there and think sometimes."

"Are you taking me to a make out spot, Mr. McBride?" she asked, teasing.

"I would never," I said as I put my hands on her waist and leaned down. I shouldn't. But I did anyway. "If you're open to it, I do have a blanket."

She grinned but didn't say anything. In answer, I kissed her cheek, ignoring the wolf whistle from one of my workers, and helped her get on the horse. She wasn't as shaky as she was the first time, and as she settled into the saddle, she gave a wary look over at Lightning, who was practically prancing in his ring.

"Do you think he's mad at me for not going over to him instead?" Jamie asked.

I nodded at the horse who I swore winked back at me.

"No. He lets Gwen on him, as well as my brothers, but he's only for experienced riders. Livvy will never get near him."

"Well I'll wave as we walk by. Or trot."

My lips tilted into a smile. "There will be no trotting. Don't worry. I'm not going to let your ass get sore."

She raised a brow. "I have a joke, but I won't say it."

"I forget you were raised with three brothers."

"And the girls in our family tell just as many dirty jokes. Just saying."

"Hey, I lived with Gwen for much of my life. I know."

I squeezed her calf and did my best to ignore the way she licked her lips. It was going to be a very hard ride for my cock if I didn't calm him down. I swung up onto my horse, settled him as I patted Giuseppe's neck, and then we were off.

"Rose has a crush on Giuseppe, so she'll follow along. As long as you do what I taught you, you'll be fine on this ride."

"I love Rose. She's so pretty." I looked over as she leaned down to run her hand down Rose's neck. "And I can see why she has a crush on Giuseppe. He's very handsome."

Giuseppe, obviously having heard her, swung his head, letting his mane flow in the wind.

I snorted. "Show off."

"Hey, you're handsome too."

"A guy needs to hear that every so often," I teased. I reached, squeezed her hand and then continued.

I didn't do this. I didn't take rides in the afternoon for a lunch date, especially with a woman who would be leaving in two weeks. But I wanted to spend as much time with her as possible. It didn't make any sense, but I didn't think it was supposed to. Not in this moment.

"Okay, what's your favorite spoon," Jamie asked after a moment.

I frowned, looking over at her as we continued our ride. We were twenty minutes into our date, talking about everything and nothing, and I wanted to soak up every bit of knowledge of her.

"Spoon?"

"Do you like the big spoon, or little spoon, what is your favorite?"

"Are we talking about sex and cuddling? Because I'm the big spoon. Though, I wouldn't mind being the little spoon every once in a while." I winked as I said it, and she burst out laughing.

"Good to know. But I meant like a metal spoon. I like a small spoon. But my brother needs to have the big soup spoon. It makes no sense to me. He's weird."

"I don't know if I've ever thought about my favorite spoon. But I guess one that can hold food rather than so flat that it feels like a fork without tines? I don't know."

"See? What your favorite spoon is says a lot about you."

"And what does it say about me?" I asked, honestly curious.

"I have no idea. I'll have to go look that one up."

I exhaled and then nodded towards the horizon. "The creek's up that way. We'll stop there for lunch…and maybe a nap."

"This nap meaning making out? Because you're going to have to be a lot less subtle."

"You are ridiculous."

"Am I? You can't stop touching me. And we're on two different horses."

"Oh. I didn't even realize." I looked down, and my hand was indeed on her thigh as we rode side by side. I coughed, and went to release my hand, but she reached out and squeezed.

"I'm blaming Rose and Giuseppe. They enjoy the cuddling."

"I guess they do."

I let go of her hand so she could handle the reins better, and we made our way around the edge of the lake as we asked each other more questions.

Favorite subject in school.

What color folder went with geography versus math.

Biggest fear.

First kiss.

First time.

Favorite type of pasta.

Favorite movie.

Favorite organizational office supply.

Favorite constellation.

Little things and everything.

We'd had six months of texting to learn this, and now in person we dug even deeper.

It was going to be hard to watch her walk away, but I wasn't going to think about that. Not right now. I was just going to feel good.

We made it to the picnic spot, and I let our horses graze, both nearly cuddling to the point that I was glad that Giuseppe was a gelding.

I set up a blanket underneath the tree so the sun wouldn't be too much, and Jamie and I worked on pulling out the cold fried chicken, potato salad, cornbread, and chocolate cake.

"My word. This is amazing."

"I think there's some carrot sticks and fruit in here as well, but I'm really here for the chicken and cake."

"I don't know. This cornbread smells amazing."

"My mom makes it in a cast iron skillet, while Cindy, our cook, bakes it in muffin cups so it's easier to travel with. I love them both."

I leaned against the tree as she knelt next to me, and we ate, and I tried to ignore the way that she groaned with each bite.

"I'm going to be so full. But I don't care."

"Riding a horse is a workout."

"Oh?" she asked. "No wonder I'm sore."

"Are you too sore? Did we go too far?" I asked, worry etched in each word.

She shook her head. "I'm fine."

"Really?" I leaned forward and brushed her pink and blonde hair from her face. "I don't want to hurt you, Jamie."

She swallowed hard and turned her head to kiss my palm. "I'm fine. Really."

"Well, if you're sore though, I could help you out there."

"Are you telling me you're good with your hands?" she teased and moved away, working to clean up our lunch. I snorted, and helped her put everything away, before I reached out and hooked her by her waist. "Sharp." A small smile played on those lips I wanted to taste.

"Well, I had to be good with my words, and my hands."

Then my mouth was on hers, and I couldn't think.

I let my hands roam over her ass, squeezing gently. When she gasped, I bit her bottom lip.

"Sore?"

"A little."

"I'll take care of you."

She pushed my hair from my face this time, as she hovered over me. I found myself on my back, her straddling me. All thoughts left my brain.

"What are we doing, Sharp?"

"Just living."

"I can't stop thinking about you."

"I don't want to stop thinking about you."

And then, without words, we promised ourselves we wouldn't think about the future, just in this moment.

I licked the seam of her lips, and she opened for me. When I ran my hand up her back to tangle in her hair, she groaned, and we deepened the kiss. She rocked over my hips, and I shifted so the heat of her rubbed against my hard cock, even though both of us wore jeans. She tossed her head back and moaned, increasing the friction.

I grinned at her, letting my hands slide up and down her sides to cup her breasts.

"We keep rubbing like that, I'm going to come in my jeans like a teenager."

Her breath came in pants, and she looked down at me, swallowing hard. "We can't have that."

And then I rolled over her, needing her.

"Want me to stop?"

"Don't stop, Sharp. Please. I need you inside me."

I closed my eyes and moaned and counted to three. That's as far as I could go. "I've been waiting for those words for far too long."

"It's just us, right here, right? You and me. No one else?"

The hesitancy in her tone nearly broke me, but I swallowed hard and nodded.

"Just you and me." And then I was kissing her again, our hands reaching for each other. I knelt between her legs and stripped off my shirt, loving the way her gaze widened.

"Oh. I guess ranch work is good for your body."

"I'm covered in scars and ink, but yeah, it's okay."

"More than okay." She reached up and played

with the single barbell in my nipple. "And how did I not know this was there?"

"It's relatively new."

I winked and then leaned down to kiss her again. When she arched her back for me, I stripped off her shirt, groaning at the way her breasts overfilled her bra.

"So fucking beautiful."

I kissed the globes of her breasts, and then undid the front snap, loving the way that her tits fell into my hands, overfilling them. Her nipples were hard little peaks that begged for my mouth. So I did what I'd wanted to do for months, and covered her nipple with my mouth, laving at her with my tongue as I used my other hand to squeeze and pluck at her nipple until she was writhing beneath me, my one thigh between her legs rubbing against the seam of her jeans over her clit. And when she arched for me, I moved to her other breast, paying it just as much attention.

And then my name was on her lips as she came, gasping against me.

"Look at you, so fucking beautiful."

"I cannot believe I just came like that," she whispered.

"I can make it better."

Then I was kissing down her body, licking and sucking as she ran her hands through my hair. I undid the button of her jeans and tugged, remembering belatedly she still wore her boots.

But I didn't care. Instead, I shoved them down and knelt between her legs even though I couldn't spread her far enough.

"This is going to be a little difficult."

"We'll manage," I growled. And then my mouth was on her pussy, tasting until I could barely hold on. Scrambling, I removed the rest of her clothes, nearly shaking with need.

I hooked one thigh over my shoulder as I dove deeper, spearing her with two fingers. As she leaned up on her forearms to look down at me, I gazed into her eyes and then spit over her cunt.

"Mine," I growled.

"Sharp," she gasped.

And then I went back to sucking and eating her out until I knew this was my feast. My essence. I speared her with three fingers, curling them so I could find her g-spot, and when she finally came again, I kept going, loving the way she rocked against my mouth, flooding me with her orgasm. As I pulled away, sucking my fingers, she looked up at me, her body flushed, her eyes wide.

"Whoa."

"I can't help it. I like the way that you taste," I growled.

Before I could say anything else, she was sitting up and tugging on my belt. Her hands shook, and I helped her undo my belt and my jeans, and she shoved my pants below my hips.

With wide eyes, she reached out, gripped my cock at the base, and pumped once, twice. I was already so hard that the vein on the underside of my dick pulsated, and pre-cum drizzled at the tip.

"Jamie, if you keep touching me like that, I'm not going to last. I'm going to come on those pretty tits, and it's going to be over soon."

"Well, you're just going to have to be strong."

And with that, she leaned forward and took me into her mouth.

My hands tangled in her hair as she ran her tongue over my cock, sliding her mouth in a way that made me see stars. She kept moving, her wet heat edging me to the point that I nearly came. She opened her mouth wider, flattening her tongue, and I couldn't help it. I shoved my cock down her throat, letting my hips flex. She gagged but didn't pull away. Instead, she gripped my hips and somehow got my dick even farther down her throat.

And then she swallowed, and I nearly came. I crossed my eyes and counted to ten, all while watching her bob along my cock, nearly sending me over the edge.

At the last moment I pulled out and squeezed my dick.

"I need to come inside that the pussy of yours. Next time. Next time your tits. And your throat."

"Next time." She met my gaze, and I hoped to hell there would be a next time.

I reached into my jeans pocket and pulled out the condom I had put there, hoping for this. She didn't say a damn thing, because I knew she had been hoping for it as well. There was no denying it.

Even though both of our jeans were still technically on, I pushed her to her back, rolled her over, and tilted her ass up slightly. And then in another moment, I was inside her, sliding into that wet heat to the point that both of us moaned out loud. She was so tight, so fucking tight that I knew I was hurting her, stretching her. But I rubbed her ass, massaging those muscles as she met me thrust for thrust.

I leaned over her, biting into her shoulder as I pumped in and out of her, her cunt squeezing my dick to the point of near pain, but I couldn't help it,

I rode her until both of us were calling out each other's names, sweat slicking us, and in that next moment I knew I needed to see her. So I pulled out of her, ignoring her moan of displeasure, and went to my back.

We maneuvered so she could straddle me, both of us tangled in boots and jeans, and then she was over me, letting me thrust deeply into her cunt to the hilt.

She rode me with her tits bouncing, both of us shaking, and there were no more words.

And when she finally came again, my thumb gliding over her clit, she fell on top of me, holding me for dear life as she shook, and I slammed into her once more, groaning her name and coming. I filled the condom to the point that I was afraid it would burst, and there was no more thinking. Just her and me in this moment.

And knowing that I never wanted to let go.

I'd marked her as mine, filled her as mine.

And when she walked away, I would be the one left behind. Marked, broken, and knowing that this might've been a mistake, but a blessed one.

One I would make again.

CHAPTER SIX

Sharp

3 days later

1

"Do you know what the fuck you're doing?" Ewan asked, and I froze, wondering where the hell that had come from.

I set down my tack and stared at Ewan. He looked the same as ever, his hair a little long, curling at the ends, his beard a little bushier since we were in the middle of the season, and Livvy and Amelia seemed to like it.

But he was still my big brother. The quieter one. The one who went all in with friendships, relationships, and family.

And I knew what he wanted. Why he was concerned.

Because I was just as concerned. Only I was doing my best to pretend I wasn't. That it made no sense. That I could live in this idea of bliss and harmony without thinking the worst.

Or perhaps I was crazy in denial. Because honestly, that might be the only thing I could do to breathe in this moment.

"Of course, I don't know what the hell I'm doing. If I knew what I was doing, I wouldn't be in the barn, cleaning up, dragging my feet because I know it's the last night she's here."

Ewan cursed under his breath and then ran his hands through his hair. "I'm not going to say that I don't want you to hurt her, or that I'll kick your ass if you do. Because she's my family, and I care about her."

I turned to look at my brother once again, that kick in the gut from his words unexpected.

"You're not?" I let out of breath. "I thought

you'd be warning me away from her because you knew it was a mistake."

"It's up to you both if you think it's a mistake. But you're my brother, Sharp. You do realize that, right? We're blood. We're family. And while I love and like Jamie, and she's my sister now, or I guess cousin, who knows how the fuck Montgomery's do family trees."

My lips twitch. "I think they're even like second cousins once removed or something like that. I have no idea how genealogy works."

"Isn't that the study of rocks?" Galen asked as he came forward, playing the bill of his hat.

I met Ewan's gaze and held back a groan. "I can't with you, Galen. It hurts. Physically hurts."

"I'm just fucking with you. I know genealogy is the study of women named Jean."

"You're an asshole." But the laughter had been needed, and I knew Galen had done it on purpose.

"So. What are you two going to do? She leaves tomorrow, bruh."

Another kick to the solar plexus. "I know she leaves tomorrow. She knows she leaves tomorrow."

"You guys haven't talked about it?" Ewan asked.

"When? When we were sneaking around, me taking her out on dates, and both of us pretending that it wasn't happening? When we were texting each other before she even got here? When I realized that I had never loved Jo and I have no idea what I'm feeling about Jamie? Is that what you mean?"

"Pretty much," Galen said, and I pinched the bridge of my nose.

"I don't know what I'm doing. Because I wasn't supposed to fall for her. I wasn't supposed to text her back. Think about her. Or want her like I do. And now I don't know what the fuck I'm supposed to do."

"Well, brother of mine. Would you leave Clover Lake for her?" Ewan asked, his voice so low that it barely carried. Galen froze next to me, and I swallowed hard.

"I don't know. It hasn't been long enough, right? I don't know what she feels for me. What she wants."

"Have you talked to her?" Both Ewan and I looked over at Galen at his words. He held up both hands. "What? I may be an idiot, but I do realize that communication is the best way to keep a relationship going. That's probably why I haven't been in a relationship. But I digress. Have you talked?"

"We've done our best not to talk," I said after a moment.

The silence between us was an answer in itself.

"Just keep in mind that the Montgomerys are like the mob."

I blinked at Ewan's words. "What?"

"They're like the mob. Once you're in, you're in. There is no getting out. But they're nice. And they have cheese. I like them. They're my family too. And if the situation had been reversed, and if Livvy hadn't wanted to move here, I wouldn't be here. You three would have to deal with the family legacy, or we'd shop it off to one of the cousins, because I would go anywhere for her. She wanted to be here, and Amelia loves it here. I got so fucking lucky."

I didn't have anything to say about that, because that meant I would have to talk to Jamie about it, and we were both so good about not doing so, that we were fucking everything up.

After a moment, they both left me to my own demons, and I finished cleaning up, knowing I needed to get back to the main house. We were having a goodbye dinner for Jamie, because she would be going home. Back to her job, her family, her life.

It wasn't supposed to be like this. It wasn't

supposed to feel as if we were ripping each other apart. And yet, time had no meaning, and I didn't want her to go.

But how selfish would it be for me to ask.

I was a rancher. I had no idea what the hell I would do in Denver. I didn't have skills that would translate down there. But maybe I could figure it out. After all, Ewan had said he would move down there. Maybe he would have a plan. I would just take his and figure it out.

With a sigh, I ran my hands over my face and made my way out of the barn so I could go to Jamie's goodbye party and pretend I wasn't breaking inside.

A shadow crossed my way, and I froze, looking up to see someone I hadn't expected.

My hands fisted at my sides as William stood there, hands in his pockets, rocking back on his heels.

"Is there some reason that you're on my property right now? Because I have the feeling the last time you were here, you tried to kill me."

I hadn't meant to say it so bluntly, but here I was, being a fucking idiot. Part of me wanted to search for a weapon, to make sure that William didn't have another chance to hurt me, and yet, the look on William's face, I wasn't sure that would've helped.

"I deserve that. I'm sorry."

I froze, wondering if perhaps he had knocked me out and this was an odd dream.

"Run that by me again?"

"I'm sorry. I know you always suspected it, but it was me. I gave you one of my grandma's sleeping pills, and I didn't realize it would knock you out so hard. I went with the prescription directions and everything. But Jo didn't know how to walk out on the wedding, to say no, and I would do anything for her. Still would. I realize that I could have killed you. Or you could have gotten hurt while you were on the side of the road, or some other shit. If you want to go to the sheriff and tell them what I did, you can. I'll take the punishment. But I don't think I can sleep anymore and be a dad and have them know what I did without me paying the consequences. Without you knowing."

Of everything that he had told me, one word stuck out, and my jaw dropped.

"A dad?"

William winced. "Jo is pregnant. We're going to be parents. She's so fucking happy. And hopefully the baby will keep her family off your back. I'm sorry about that. I know I'm an asshole. I know that I'm not a good person, and I'm working on it. For my kid. I'll work on it. And I know Jo will too. But I'm sorry. For hurting you, and for not having the balls to stand up for the woman that I love. For not telling her family that I wanted to be the one to love her. They only wanted her to marry you because they wanted your family name. And I guess that's what she was going for too. I'm nobody compared to the McBrides. And I let that get to me. I let a lot of things get to me in the past. So I'm sorry. I have a feeling that the family will stop messing with your woman now, and you. They're going to focus on us. And I wanted you to know. So anything you want to do, you let me know. I'll take it. I deserve it. I'm sorry."

Out of all of the scenarios I had played over in my mind when it came to this moment or finding out for sure what William had done, this had never entered the space. The idea that William would be so open. So truthful. If it wasn't for the fact that I had grown up with this guy, and knew his face, his mannerisms, his voice, I would've said that he was a doppelganger or some shit. But no, this was him. And perhaps I was losing my damn mind.

"You could have killed me."

"I know," he said with a wince. "I couldn't think of anything else, and I guess I watched too many movies. Sorry."

"I want to say that sorry is not good enough, but frankly, you're the one who has to deal with that family day in and day out. Maybe that's cruel of me, but maybe you did me a favor."

I couldn't believe I was saying these words. I had been so mad at him for so long, even before the wedding, and yet, I couldn't take it out on him. Not when it felt like it was a lifetime ago.

"What?"

"I can't forgive you. Because that was so fucking stupid. It was idiotic. And dangerous. And if I hear about you doing anything similar, or if I hear that your kid's ever in danger? I'll go to the sheriff. I'll go to the media. Or I'll kick your ass. And maybe you helped me in the long run. Albeit in the most idiotic and criminally way possible."

William blanched, but nodded in agreement. "I'm in your debt."

"Maybe. Just be a good dad, okay? And make sure Jo's a good mom. And make sure that they don't fuck with my family."

"That I'll do. I'll stand up to them. Jo's brothers are assholes, but I'll do it. For my kid."

"Do it for yourself too."

"You McBrides were always decent."

"I thought we were righteous assholes?" I asked wryly.

"Maybe. But I'm the idiot who's lucked out. So, I guess I'll go. But good luck. And congrats with your new woman. You guys seem happy around town."

I didn't smile, didn't say anything, just tilted my head in a silent goodbye, and then William walked to his truck parked at the end of the drive, and I didn't have the heart to say that Jamie wasn't mine.

That this was our last night.

Unless we figured something out. Long distance could work, right? We had to talk, had to figure it out.

But first I needed to see her.

I took a few steps towards the house, and Galen stood there, slack jawed. "You just let him go? He just said that he tried to kill you."

"He didn't try to kill me. Just tried to stop me from marrying the love of his life."

"Did you hit your head or something? How could you just let him go?"

"Because it'll bring it all up again. It'll hurt this family. It'll hurt Jamie. And I don't care. Jo and

William are each other's problems, and if William can get his head out of his ass, maybe the McBrides won't have to deal with them anymore. And maybe that kid won't be fucked up."

"Well, that's a nice image. Seriously though, you're a better man than me."

My lips twitched. "I would say something snarky on that, but we both know you're a decent guy, bruh," I said, drawing out the word.

"You're an idiot. Seriously. An idiot. Come on, let's go see your woman."

I flinched. "What if she doesn't want to be my woman."

"The first step is admitting you have a problem. Maybe admitting your feelings. I know it's hard."

"Fuck," I growled, as we made our way into the house, and I couldn't help but freeze at the doorway.

Jamie stood near my mom, both of them looking over a tablet, going over something having to do with the calendar.

She'd been helping with a few things around the ranch in the past week, helping manage our time-line, since Gwen hated doing it, but it had been her job along with multiple other things for the past few years. But there Jamie was, making it seem so fucking simple.

It was amazing. And I didn't know how to tell her what I felt. Because I didn't know what I felt.

Galen gave me a look like I was crazy. Before I could say anything, Jamie looked up at me and smiled.

That smile hit me like a brick to the chest, and I swallowed hard.

"Hey."

"Hey."

My mother smiled between us and took the tablet from Jamie's hands. "Why don't you two go for a walk while we work on dinner. That way we can make your party special."

Now my parents were full on pushing and matchmaking, and I couldn't be more grateful. I held up my hand, ignoring Livvy's worried look, and took Jamie's hand in mine.

"Just a little walk."

"Will you take me for a walk too, Uncle Sharp?" Amelia asked, and I looked down at my niece and knelt.

"Soon. You're my best girl." I kissed Amelia's cheeks, and she smiled at me.

"Just like Aunt Jamie."

As everyone in the room laughed, even Jamie and me, Ameilia skipped her way to her parents, and I dragged Jamie out of the room before I could embarrass us even further.

We walked in silence, hand in hand until we were at the edge of the barn area, watching Lightning run around his paddock before Franklin made him head to the stall.

"Did I ever say thank you for working with my mom on that management software? It's been killing us since our old software went out of date, and while we're decent at it, you're brilliant."

Jamie rolled her eyes. "It's what I use for Montgomery Builders. Tabby uses something slightly different, but we each have our own favorite thing. Seriously, it's what I do for a living, and I enjoy it. I freelance sometimes for other companies, so I told your mom if she needs help in the future, I'm here."

I shuddered out a breath and pushed her hair back from her face. The wind picked up slightly, and I knew she was probably regretting not putting her hair up. It was little things like that that I knew.

Maybe I had already fallen. Hard.

"I'm glad. That you'll be working with us."

"Yeah. I always want to help. I know that you're working so hard with making sure the horse section of the McBride Ranch gets up and running, and I was looking at your paperwork, and you really have it down. You're going to do amazing."

"Yeah? Maybe I need you to keep looking at my paperwork."

"I can do that."

"So you love working with Montgomery Builders?" I blurted, hating myself.

A sad expression covered her face, and she nodded. "I do. I love working with my family. And other companies." She paused and looked down at her joined hands. "I love the space that it gives me. Because one day I want to take time for myself too. See the world like some of my cousins have done. Have a family. Be a mom. Which is crazy because I don't have kids and I can't believe I just said that out loud."

I laughed. I couldn't help it. "Tonight's been a night for revelations, hasn't it?" A pause. "I don't want you to go."

"I don't want to go either. But I have to be back tomorrow. I have meetings. Appointments. My life is in Denver, Sharp. I wasn't supposed to want to stay."

I wiped a tear from her cheek and swallowed hard so I wouldn't cry right with her.

"Can long distance work? Us figuring out how to visit? Our lives are so different, but every time I'm near you, I can breathe again."

"Maybe. I...I don't want to go. But I need to. It can't be forever, but I also...I just need to think." Her smile went wobbly, and she ran her hands down my chest. "But right now I'm going to have to be the runaway this time."

And she went to her toes, kissed me softly on the mouth, and turned.

"Jamie."

"Can I have a minute? Just a minute. I need to breathe, and if I look at you right now, I'm not going to want to leave, I just need to think."

I reached for her, slid my hand down her back, but she didn't turn towards me.

I knew if she did, I wouldn't let go, and we'd break. We'd step away from our responsibilities, and into this fantasy of a connection that might not make sense.

So instead, I stood there as she walked away, and I hoped to hell she would come back.

Chapter Seven

Jamie

My chest ached, but I told myself that I was fine. Overreacting.

Just because I was leaving in less than twenty-four hours and didn't have a plan, didn't mean that I needed to start crying. I wrapped my arms around myself, the wind picking up a bit. I knew that there were storms predicted for later, but I still had a couple of hours, and I couldn't help but remember the first time that I had met Sharp. The storm that had come out of nowhere. I didn't want to want him. I didn't want to fall in love and figure out what the hell I wanted because if I did, it felt as if the worst could happen.

Or maybe I was wrong. Maybe I just needed to breathe again.

What did it mean that I couldn't stop thinking about him. That I wanted to see what would happen in the future. It couldn't be anything. Because he wasn't mine. And there really wasn't an easy way out of this. I knew life wasn't easy, but we only had known each other for so few weeks. Yes, we'd had a month with each other here, a month of stolen kisses and moments in each other's arms, but was that enough to uproot my life? Because I would have to be the one who did so. I wouldn't force him to leave his family and his ranch. He had just started a whole new side to the family business. He couldn't up and move his horses and cattle to Denver. But maybe I could do my job here. Yet, that was moving so fast. He hadn't even asked me to stay. He'd asked about long distance. Had said he didn't want me to go, but with no real plan behind it.

My phone buzzed, and part of me wanted it to be him, to check on me, even though I had just walked away so I could breathe.

But as I slid out my phone, tears pricked my eyes, and I answered.

"Mom."

"Baby. What's wrong? Where are you?"

"I'm fine." Then I promptly burst into tears.

I didn't know what was wrong with me. This wasn't the end of the world. It wasn't life or death. It was a decision that didn't need to be made now, and yet I had done my best not to think about feelings for so long that I couldn't help but want to think about them.

"Who do I have to hurt?" Colin asked, as he leaned against Mom in the frame, and frowned. "Do you need me to drive up there? I will. No, we have friends with planes, I'll go find one."

"I'm fine," I said. "I love you all. I promise. I'm just having feelings."

"Did that asshole hurt you?" Colin asked, his voice low.

"What?"

"Jamie. You do realize that you are living with our cousin, who talks to me. And a few of us. And every time that you check in, you mention a certain someone." Colin shook his head, as if disappointed I hadn't thought about it.

I looked at my mother, who gave me a knowing look. "Baby. What's going on between you and Sharp?"

"I don't know. That's the problem. I don't know what's going on between us or what we want to happen between us. I'm leaving tomorrow, Mom. I'm heading home to go back to work, and back to my life and to my apartment, and to act as if nothing happened, and yet part of me is going to break apart once I get there. But Denver is my home. You're my home. And just the fact that I'm thinking about changing something or taking a drastic step after so little time scares me."

"Have you and Sharp talked about it at all?"

"I think he wants me to stay. He said something about a long-distance relationship."

"Hey, that's good. That's voicing some desire of the future," Colin said, slight hope in his voice. But he also had his phone in his hand, and I narrowed my gaze at him. "Do not go into the group chat or look up flights."

"I'm doing nothing of the kind," he obviously lied.

"Colin, let your sister handle this. What do you want, baby girl?"

I wanted to say something but shook my head, unsure. "I don't know. I don't want this to end, but I don't know of a path that's not going to hurt somebody. Or have us make changes that we're not ready for."

"Love isn't easy."

"Nobody said anything about love, Mom."

She merely raised a brow as Colin rolled his eyes, and I let them use their silence as practical screaming.

"I just don't know, Mom. I like him a lot. I have feelings for him. We have so much in common, and he makes me laugh. He makes me smile, and I love the way that he is with his family."

"Do you like the ranch?" my mom asked, her voice so tentative I knew she was afraid of what I was going to say.

I loved my mom. I loved being near her, loved seeing her multiple times a week. I was a mama's girl. Just like I was a daddy's girl. I was a Montgomery.

"I love it here." I shook my head. "Honestly, I love learning how everything works, and I'm enjoying helping each person individually figure out how to make the family business thrive. It's so much fun, and I love watching Amelia grow up even in the short time I've been here. And Livvy is such a bright light, and she's brilliant, and I don't know, it just makes me happy to be here. And it feels weird that I'm even saying those words."

"Maybe you should tell him that. Even if it hurts. You don't have to make a decision right now, or even this week. Come home, see if distance can work, but it isn't the end if you move, or he moves, it's a choice. It's figuring out who you are to each other. And it's okay if you have to change your path. Because no matter what we will be with you. Even if we're not next door."

"And that'll give me an excuse to road trip more," Colin said with a wink. "Or if he decides to move here, it'll let me have more eyes on him. Because as soon as Leif and Gideon know what's going on, we're going to have to interrogate this man."

"Mom," I warned, and she just grinned.

"I'm not going to help you with that. You're the one that has three brothers."

"You're the one who decided to have four kids."

"That is true. I love you, baby. Be safe. The clouds look a little dark. I want you safe and home."

"I'll see you tomorrow. I love you."

"I love you too."

I hung up the phone, slid it in my pocket, and let out a breath.

I was probably a mile away from the ranch now, as I had walked in silence for so long. I started to head back and looked up into the dark sky, wondering if there was a choice for me to make.

"Give me a sign. Should I stay or go. Just a sign."

Rain started to fall in earnest in that moment, and I cursed under my breath. Well. I had no idea what that meant as an answer or a sign, but I ducked my head, trying to block most of the rain from hitting my face, and pulled out my phone.

Hail slammed into me at that moment, and I tripped over a rock, tossing my phone, and slamming my knee into the ground.

"Fuck." I staggered up, sliding in the mud that seemed to come out of nowhere, and reached for my phone.

It had cracked, the entire thing going dark, and alarm shot through me.

I was not a Wyoming girl. Not a country girl. I just needed to get back to the ranch.

I looked around, slightly disoriented. All I could see was rain, and part of the creek that was now moving far faster than it had even ten minutes ago.

"Okay, I can do this. The house was west, and

that means I make sure that the creek is on the right of me. Right?"

I wasn't in Denver where I could always know exactly where the mountains were, where the main streets were alphabetical or numbered, no, this wasn't a grid.

And now the temperature was dropping, and I kept moving, hoping to hell I knew what I was doing.

This was not the sign that I wanted.

I kept moving, the creek rising quickly, and I swallowed hard, wondering how long it would take to get back. Maybe there was shelter I could stay in along the way.

I knew storms out here were dangerous, had even been inside during one, but this was ridiculous.

Thunder cracked overhead, lightning shooting up the sky, and I ran, sliding in the mud, falling more than once, but it didn't matter. I just needed to get back. To the ranch. To Sharp.

The sound of thunder increased, but it sounded different this time. Water began to rise at my ankles, and I knew that if I wasn't careful, whatever waterway or flood was coming would take me. I wasn't even sure I was going the right way.

"Jamie!" a voice called through the wind, and I

closed my eyes, trying to blink through the rain, but hail kept slicing into my skin, leaving bloody patches and bruises.

"Sharp!" I called back over the rain.

"Jamie!"

Water began to come in earnest, the creek over-filling as a wave came down, the water rising out of nowhere.

"Jamie. I've got you."

And then out of nowhere, Sharp was there, rain slick, and riding Lightning. The horse reared, hooves in the air, and I covered my face, unsure that either one of them could see me.

And then Sharp was off the horse and holding me.

"Okay, Lightning is strong enough to take us both. Get on the horse, baby. I've got you." He ran his hands over my body, and I winced.

"How did you find me?"

"I will always find you, Jamie." Then he crushed his mouth to mine and held me close, even as the water began to rise.

"We have to hurry. Come on."

Everything moved quickly after that, and suddenly I was on the back of Lightning with Sharp behind me, and then the horse was moving.

The water was still rising though not where we were going, and Lightning moved with such quickness and grace, that everything felt as if we were in a dream.

Nothing felt real, and my teeth chattered, and the small cuts on my body stung, but I leaned forward as Sharp told me to, and knew that the heat of him behind me would be my solace.

The rain continued to pour even as we made it to the edge of the property.

He didn't take me to either one of the homes, instead to the barn, as we bounded through the open doors, lightning and heavy winds billowing behind us.

People were moving all around, keeping the animals safe, closing windows and protecting the property, but I felt like I was drugged, moving steps behind as Sharp jumped off Lightning and pulled me with.

"I've got you, baby. I've got you."

"You found me." I shook my head. "That storm came out of nowhere."

"Welcome to Wyoming." The worry in his gaze nearly broke me, but before I could say anything, I turned and put both of my hands on Lightning's flank.

"Thank you, buddy. You're so beautiful. I'm sorry for scaring us both when I first met you."

Tears fell down my face, but I knew it was just the adrenaline.

Other people were saying things. Even as Franklin and Gavin took Lightning away, I swore the horse winked at me, but maybe I was just delusional and shivering.

Sharp wrapped a blanket around me, and I just stared up at him, blinking.

"You're okay. Right? Do I need to get a doctor?"

"I'm fine. Although I didn't realize that hail hurt so much."

"I shouldn't have let you go off on your own."

"We didn't know the storm was going to be that quick. I feel like an idiot, and I broke my phone." I pulled my phone out of my pocket, and he took it, shaking his head before putting in his back pocket.

"I'll get you a new one."

"You don't have to, Sharp."

"Hell yes I do. My ranch tried to kill you."

"I didn't realize that flash floods were so, well, quick. I realize it's in the name, but wow."

"The creek rises like that in that one spot, but it doesn't come near the ranch. That's why I didn't even think about it. I didn't know you'd go so far. But I wasn't thinking. And that was the problem."

"Thank you. Thanks for saving me. Though I kind of wish I could have not been a damsel and saved myself."

"You were coming back. You were going the right direction, and you weren't panicking. You were getting here. You would've saved yourself. Lightning and I just wanted to be the heroes."

"I'm getting that horse all the sugar cubes he wants."

"Damn straight."

He pushed my hair back from my face and rubbed his thumbs along my jaw.

"I'm so sorry. You scared the hell out of me."

"I was pretty scared too."

And then he lowered his lips to mine, and I was lost.

I didn't know what would happen next, but I knew what I wanted.

Him.

And it hadn't taken an act of God for that to happen.

But as he pulled back, I ran my hands up and down his chest, mostly trying to stay warm and needing to touch him.

"Right before it started to rain I asked the gods for a sign if I should stay or go."

Sharp winced. "I guess a flash flood and storm out of nowhere with a tornado warning probably isn't a good sign."

"Maybe they sent me you though?" I asked softly, and his smile was so bright, that I nearly fell to my knees right there and then.

"Yeah?"

"Maybe. I don't know what's going to happen, Sharp. But I don't want this to be the end. You and I seem to have a thing for rain."

"So give me a chance? Whether it's here or there, I don't want to let go."

"Then don't."

And as Livvy and his family came into the barn, all with worried tones and outstretched arms, I held onto Sharp and let him kiss me.

"I love you," he whispered against my ear.

I smiled, my hands shaking. "I love you too."

And as the others tried to pull us away, checking for injuries and speaking all at once, I met Sharp's gaze, and knew that I might be returning home soon, but in the end, Sharp would be my home.

No matter where we stayed, ended up, or found our future.

He was my accidental everything.

Epilogue

Sharp

The sun glowed red behind my eyelids, and I forced my eyes open, knowing it was going to be a little too bright. I squinted, then rolled my shoulders back, knowing today was going to be a long day. Thankfully, we had a plan, and I could get away at the end a little bit early if I hedged my bets.

I groaned, feeling far different today than I had the first time I had done this.

After all, it wasn't every day that a man needed to head to a church for his wedding.

Of course, we weren't going to an actual church this time. We weren't taking any chances with anything being too similar to the first time I had been thrown into this.

"Okay, you have your tux on, you're wearing your boots, we have your fancy hat because of course you need the fancy hat for the wedding, that way everybody can still be surprised when you go bald later."

"Seriously?" I asked, as Gwen began to pace, checking off points on her list, on her actual godforsaken clipboard. It was an odd rose-gold color that matched the wedding colors that Jamie and I had chosen, and she was in full wedding-planning mode. It didn't matter that we'd hired an actual planner who worked with the ranch often, since everybody had full-time jobs, sometimes two in Jamie's case, but Gwen needed to be a part of it.

I loved my baby sister. Though she was annoying the fuck out of me right now.

"I do not have a receding hairline."

"So you say. But if you wear your hat enough, you're not going to truly see it."

"I'm not always wearing the hat."

"No, sometimes you wear your ball cap." Galen winked at me as he played with the rim of his own hat. "Not to mention, I heard the girls saying that guys looked hotter when they wore their hat backwards. So remember that if you and Jamie ever fight and you need to get out of something."

"That's your advice? Put your hat backwards so you could what, swoon the anger out of her?" Ewan asked with a cluck of his tongue.

"What? It sounds like a good plan."

"At this point I'm taking notes. The Montgomerys can be scary." I held up my fist, and Ewan bonked it, shaking his head. "They enjoy us saying that, or I'd hide from everybody for even daring to use those words."

"I wonder if there's a Montgomery cousin for me," Galen said as he ran his hand over his newly shaved face. We all usually wore beards, but he'd shaved it to try something different. When I had called him an infant, saying that he looked like a ballsac, he punched me. But that was what brothers were for.

"By the way, do not touch any one of Jamie or Livvy's cousins," I ordered Galen.

My brother held up both hands. "What? Are you telling me they're off limits? Because telling me they're off limits is a problem."

"I love that you act like you're some playboy,

when you're nothing of the sort," Gwendolyn said, as she pointed her pen at him. "But seriously, don't touch a Montgomery cousin this weekend. We want *this* wedding to actually go off without a hitch."

The way that she emphasized the word *this* made me narrow my gaze. "We are all aware that the first wedding wasn't my fault, right?"

"The way that it ended up? No," Ewan began.

"But the fact that you were even going to marry that woman to begin with?" Gwen shook her head. "That's all on you."

My shoulders fell. "Fine. I promise I won't be stupid again."

"Can you please write that on your handy-dandy clipboard?" Galen asked, tapping his fingers on the edge of the chair. "We need to make sure that everybody remembers that."

"Then why is everyone picking on me? It's my wedding day."

"It's Jamie's wedding day. You just happen to be there." Gwendolyn frowned. "Or at least, I hope you get there. Okay, each of us will be driving, and we'll have Ewan in the front, leading. I'll be in the center with the spare truck just in case we run out of gas or something, and Galen will be taking up the rear, just in case both trucks fail. And Galen, if you make a taking-up-the-rear joke right now, I will throw my fancy clipboard at you."

Galen shut his mouth, his eyes dancing, and I met Ewan's gaze.

I loved my family, I really did. The McBrides were something else, and when you added all our cousins together? Well, we couldn't rival the Montgomerys, but we came pretty close.

"I will walk through fire to get to this wedding. And we're getting married at the creek right along the edge of the property. I'm not going to be late, I'm not going to miss out. I'm going to marry Jamie Montgomery, and there's nothing anyone can do about it."

"That's what I like to hear," a deep voice said from behind me, and I whirled to see the big, tatted, and bearded Austin Montgomery practically filling up the doorway.

"Sir. Well. I'm glad you heard that part of the conversation," I said with a laugh.

"I figured you might be nervous, but I'm pretty nervous too. Giving away my baby girl isn't easy."

Galen whistled beneath his breath, and I resisted the urge to steal Gwen's clipboard and throw it at him.

"I'm just grateful that Jamie said yes. Because

we both know if you were actually going to give her away, she'd run down the aisle because she doesn't believe anyone can give her away."

"That's my baby girl. I'm just here to make sure that you get to the ceremony. In fact, do you mind riding with me? You know, just so we could have that father, son-in-law time?"

Panic nearly seeped in, and I heard more than saw Ewan and Galen fist-bump each other, and I swallowed hard.

"No problem. As long as I get to Jamie, that's fine with me."

"Good. Are you guys ready?"

"All ready to go," Gwen said as she tapped her clipboard. "You guys will stay up front, and we've got a plan. We'll just have Ewan follow you, and we'll make it to the wedding in no time. Now, we have our hats, suits, and I look amazing in my suit, by the way," she said as she slid her hands down her hips. "And because I know if I even look at a Montgomery man in any sort of way my brothers will murder them, I'll just have to find a townie."

"Finding someone in Clover Lake isn't going to help you either," Ewan snarled, and I just shook my head, before following Austin to his truck.

They'd driven up from Denver, and I was

forever grateful that these were going to be my in-laws. They were hilarious, caring, and brought an exorbitant amount of cheese. I didn't quite understand it, but I didn't mind. I'd learn to love cheese with the quiet abandon that they did.

I slid into the truck, my knees shaking. "Come on, let's do this."

"Nervous?"

"Just a little. Then again, I think I just want to get there, make sure there isn't an act of God trying to separate us, and get through my vows without stumbling."

"As someone who made more than a few mistakes back in my day, I understand that. But you're taking my heart with you. I hope you know that." Austin pulled out onto the main road, our parade behind us, and I swallowed hard.

"I get it. I really do. I know I seem fickle because this is my second wedding, but I'm going to make this one work."

"You had your reasons for the first one, and I understand wanting to make the family proud. You have no idea. But I also see the way you look at my daughter. And the way that she looks at you. This just means we have more of a reason to come visit Wyoming."

I smiled then, keeping an eye out on the rolling clouds. It better not rain today.

"At some point the Montgomerys are going to outnumber the McBrides in Wyoming."

"That would be a shame," Austin teased. Then he frowned and tapped something on his dash.

"What is it?" I asked, alarm shooting through me.

"It's nothing. Well hell. Hold on." Then Austin Montgomery, my hopefully soon-to-be father-in-law, pulled to the side of the road, confusing the hell out of me.

"Austin? Are you okay? Do you need to call someone?"

"Just wait a minute. I've got this."

But he didn't do a damn thing. Instead he let the truck run idle, as Ewan, Galen, and Gwen, waved as they passed us.

"What's going on?"

"Hold on, can you get out for a second? I'll meet you around the engine."

Wondering what the hell was happening, and more than a little confused, I hopped out of the truck and closed the door. Then the damn man sped off, and I took a step back, grateful he didn't hit me.

I stared at the dust plume, open mouthed, as the

man waved at me, and kept moving down the road, following my traitorous siblings.

"What the fuck?"

They had all left me on the side of the road on my wedding day? I didn't want to reminisce about this. I wanted to be with Jamie. What the hell?

I looked both ways, not seeing a single fucking car, and realized I was going to be late. I was going to be a runaway groom not once, but twice in my life. Jamie was never going to forgive me. Hell, I was never going to forgive her father or my siblings again.

Then I turned at the sound of an engine and saw a familiar SUV driving up. My jaw fell as Jamie pulled up next to me and rolled down the window.

"Hey stranger, need a ride?"

I licked my lips, my mouth suddenly dry, as I stared at the love of my life, in a soft and lacy white gown, flowers woven into her updo'd braid.

She had her makeup all glammed out but still looked like the Jamie I loved. Her hot-pink streaks wove into her white-blonde hair perfectly, and I realized that she wore my grandmother's necklace.

"Jamie. Thought it was bad luck to see the bride before the wedding?"

"I figured it cancels out the bad luck of the

groom being left behind on his wedding day. What do you think? Am I adorable?"

"You are the sexiest, most adorable, most amazing woman I've ever met. But what the fuck?" I asked, shaking my head. "I thought your dad was going to kill me and bury me in a hole."

"We could have had any of your siblings do it, but Dad really wanted to be part of it. Now hop on in, and now I get to drive you to the wedding."

I shook my head, got into the SUV, and leaned forward, capturing her lips in a kiss that nearly sent us both over the edge.

"You're going to need to redo your makeup," I growled.

"If I didn't know for a fact that your sister had circled around and is on her way back up the road, I'd show you that I'm not actually wearing panties under this dress."

She winked as she said it, and I groaned, my dick hard, and she pulled out onto the road.

"You are a witch."

"I'm about to be your witch. Let's go get married, Sharp McBride."

"Jamie Montgomery, you are my insanity. And I love you."

"And I love you too. And I promise never to run away."

"Even accidentally," I muttered, then leaned to the side, kissed her on the cheek, and ignored all of my family as they parked on the road near the creek, honking horns and shouting at us.

I was marrying into a crazy family, but the good part was, it seemed that my family was just as insane.

It was a match made in Wyoming heaven.

The final book in the series is next with His Practically Fake Proposal!

Shep & Shae's romance, Ink Inspired, started it all. So don't miss out Livvy's parents fell in love in New Orleans!

Lexington Montgomery finds his match in Last Chance Seduction in the Montgomery Ink Legacy series! Livvy and Ewan are also part of that series and will make guest appearances.

If you'd like to read the next Generation with the Montgomery Ink Legacy Series:

Bittersweet Promises

In the mood to read another family saga? Meet the Cage Family in The Forever Rule!

In the mood for more small town romance? Check out the Ashford Creek series with LEGACY. Or as I like to call it "The Small Town of Single Dads".

A Note from Carrie Ann Ryan

Thank you so much for reading Accidental Runway Groom!

When I originally decided to write the Montgomery Ink Legacy series, I knew there would be certain Montgomerys that wanted to jump the line and get their stories first. Livvy was one of those characters. I just loved her so much and knew I needed to fit in a romance for her somewhere. Always a Fake Bridesmaid was originally supposed to be a novella in the MIL series, but then I met Ewan.

cue swooning

As soon as I figured out his backstory and ended up doing WAY too much research for a single line of dialogue and couldn't help but fall in love with a new setting and new family. I did not have time for a new series, but then again, the characters do what they want.

So welcome to Clover Lake. A brand new series of tasty romances about the McBrides.

And yes, each of the McBrides get a book… though one of them might head back to Denver. Ahem.

———

The final book in the series is next with His Practically Fake Proposal!

Shep & Shae's romance, Ink Inspired, started it all. So don't miss out Livvy's parents fell in love in New Orleans!

Lexington Montgomery finds his match in Last Chance Seduction in the Montgomery Ink Legacy series! Livvy and Ewan are also part of that series and will make guest appearances.

Clover Lake
Book 1: Always a Fake Bridesmaid (Livvy & Ewan)

Book 2: Accidental Runaway Groom (Jamie & Sharp)

Book 3: His Practically Fake Proposal (Galen & Addy)

If you want to make sure you know what's coming next from me, you can sign up for my newsletter at www.CarrieAnnRyan.com; follow me on twitter at @CarrieAnnRyan, or like my Facebook page. I also have a Facebook Fan Club where we have trivia, chats, and other goodies. You guys are the reason I get to do what I do and I thank you.

Make sure you're signed up for my MAILING LIST so you can know when the next releases are available as well as find giveaways and FREE READS.

Happy Reading!

ALSO FROM CARRIE ANN RYAN

The Montgomery Ink Legacy Series:
Book 1: Bittersweet Promises (Leif & Brooke)
Book 2: At First Meet (Nick & Lake)
Book 2.5: Happily Ever Never (May & Leo)
Book 3: Longtime Crush (Sebastian & Raven)
Book 4: Best Friend Temptation (Noah, Ford, and Greer)
Book 4.5: Happily Ever Maybe (Jennifer & Gus)
Book 5: Last First Kiss (Daisy & Hugh)
Book 6: His Second Chance (Kane & Phoebe)
Book 7: One Night with You (Kingston & Claire)
Book 8: Accidentally Forever (Crew & Aria)

Book 9: Last Chance Seduction (Lexington & Mercy)

Book 10: Kiss Me Forever (Brooklyn & Reece)

Book 11: His Guilty Pleasure (Dash & Aly)

Book 12: Maybe it's You (Riley & Gage)

The Cage Family

Book 1: The Forever Rule (Aston & Blakely)

Book 2: An Unexpected Everything (Isabella & Weston)

Book 3: If You Were Mine (Dorian & Harper)

Book 4: One Quick Obsession (Hudson & Scarlett)

Book 5: Pretend it's Forever (Sophia & Carson)

Book 6: Wish it Were You (Flynn & Luna)

Ashford Creek

Book 1: Legacy (Callum & Felicity)

Book 2: Crossroads (Bodhi & Kiera)

Book 3: Westward (Atlas & Elizabeth)

Book 4: Patience (Teagan & Rush)

Clover Lake

Book 1: Always a Fake Bridesmaid (Livvy & Ewan)

Book 2: Accidental Runaway Groom (Jamie & Sharp)

Book 3: His Practically Fake Proposal (Galen & Addy)

The Wilder Brothers Series:

Book 1: One Way Back to Me (Eli & Alexis)

Book 2: Always the One for Me (Evan & Kendall)

Book 3: The Path to You (Everett & Bethany)

Book 4: Coming Home for Us (Elijah & Maddie)

Book 5: Stay Here With Me (East & Lark)

Book 6: Finding the Road to Us (Elliot, Trace, and Sidney)

Book 7: Moments for You (Ridge & Aurora)

Book 7.5: A Wilder Wedding (Amos & Naomi)

Book 8: Forever For Us (Wyatt & Ava)

Book 9: Pieces of Me (Gabriel & Briar)

Book 10: Endlessly Yours (Brooks & Rory)

The Falling for the Cassidy Brothers Series:

(Formerly the First Time Series)

Book 1: Good Time Boyfriend (Heath & Devney)

Book 2: Last Minute Fiancé (Luca & Addison)

Book 3: Second Chance Husband (August & Paisley)

Montgomery Ink Denver:

Book 0.5: <u>Ink Inspired </u>(Shep & Shea)

Book 0.6: <u>Ink Reunited </u>(Sassy, Rare, and Ian)

Book 1: <u>Delicate Ink</u> (Austin & Sierra)

Book 1.5: <u>Forever Ink </u>(Callie & Morgan)

Book 2: <u>Tempting Boundaries </u>(Decker and Miranda)

Book 3: <u>Harder than Words </u>(Meghan & Luc)

Book 3.5: <u>Finally Found You </u>(Mason & Presley)

Book 4: <u>Written in Ink </u>(Griffin & Autumn)

Book 4.5: <u>Hidden Ink </u>(Hailey & Sloane)

Book 5: <u>Ink Enduring </u>(Maya, Jake, and Border)

Book 6: <u>Ink Exposed </u>(Alex & Tabby)

Book 6.5: <u>Adoring Ink </u>(Holly & Brody)

Book 6.6: <u>Love, Honor, & Ink </u>(Arianna & Harper)

Book 7: <u>Inked Expressions </u>(Storm & Everly)

Book 7.3: <u>Dropout </u>(Grayson & Kate)

Book 7.5: <u>Executive Ink </u>(Jax & Ashlynn)

Book 8: <u>Inked Memories</u> (Wes & Jillian)

Book 8.5: <u>Inked Nights </u>(Derek & Olivia)

Book 8.7: <u>Second Chance Ink</u> (Brandon & Lauren)

Book 8.5: Montgomery Midnight Kisses (Alex & Tabby Bonus(

Bonus: Inked Kingdom (Stone & Sarina)

Montgomery Ink: Colorado Springs

Book 1: Fallen Ink (Adrienne & Mace)

Book 2: Restless Ink (Thea & Dimitri)

Book 2.5: Ashes to Ink (Abby & Ryan)

Book 3: Jagged Ink (Roxie & Carter)

Book 3.5: Ink by Numbers (Landon & Kaylee)

The Montgomery Ink: Boulder Series:

Book 1: Wrapped in Ink (Liam & Arden)

Book 2: Sated in Ink (Ethan, Lincoln, and Holland)

Book 3: Embraced in Ink (Bristol & Marcus)

Book 3: Moments in Ink (Zia & Meredith)

Book 4: Seduced in Ink (Aaron & Madison)

Book 4.5: Captured in Ink (Julia, Ronin, & Kincaid)

Book 4.7: Inked Fantasy (Secret ??)

Book 4.8: A Very Montgomery Christmas (The Entire Boulder Family)

The Montgomery Ink: Fort Collins Series:

Book 1: Inked Persuasion (Jacob & Annabelle)

Book 2: Inked Obsession (Beckett & Eliza)

Book 3: Inked Devotion (Benjamin & Brenna)

Book 3.5: Nothing But Ink (Clay & Riggs)

Book 4: Inked Craving (Lee & Paige)

Book 5: Inked Temptation (Archer & Killian)

The Promise Me Series:

Book 1: Forever Only Once (Cross & Hazel)

Book 2: From That Moment (Prior & Paris)

Book 3: Far From Destined (Macon & Dakota)

Book 4: From Our First (Nate & Myra)

The Whiskey and Lies Series:

Book 1: Whiskey Secrets (Dare & Kenzie)

Book 2: Whiskey Reveals (Fox & Melody)

Book 3: Whiskey Undone (Loch & Ainsley)

The Gallagher Brothers Series:

Book 1: Love Restored (Graham & Blake)

Book 2: Passion Restored (Owen & Liz)

Book 3: Hope Restored (Murphy & Tessa)

The Carr Family Series:

(Formerly the Less Than Series)

Book 1: Breathless With Her (Devin & Erin)

Book 2: Reckless With You (Tucker & Amelia)

Book 3: Shameless With Him (Caleb & Zoey)

The Fractured Connections Series:

Book 1: Breaking Without You (Cameron & Violet)

Book 2: Shouldn't Have You (Brendon & Harmony)

Book 3: Falling With You (Aiden & Sienna)

Book 4: Taken With You (Beckham & Meadow)

The Campus Roommates Series:

(Formerly the On My Own Series)

Book 0.5: My First Glance

Book 1: My One Night (Dillon & Elise)

Book 2: My Rebound (Pacey & Mackenzie)

Book 3: My Next Play (Miles & Nessa)

Book 4: My Bad Decisions (Tanner & Natalie)

The Ravenwood Coven Series:

Book 1: Dawn Unearthed

Book 2: Dusk Unveiled

Book 3: Evernight Unleashed

The Aspen Pack Series:

Book 1: Etched in Honor
Book 2: Hunted in Darkness
Book 3: Mated in Chaos
Book 4: Harbored in Silence
Book 5: Marked in Flames

The Talon Pack:
Book 1: <u>Tattered Loyalties</u>
Book 2: <u>An Alpha's Choice</u>
Book 3: <u>Mated in Mist</u>
Book 4: <u>Wolf Betrayed</u>
Book 5: <u>Fractured Silence</u>
Book 6: <u>Destiny Disgraced</u>
Book 7: <u>Eternal Mourning</u>
Book 8: <u>Strength Enduring</u>
Book 9: <u>Forever Broken</u>
Book 10: Mated in Darkness
Book 11: Fated in Winter

Redwood Pack Series:
Book 0.5: <u>An Alpha's Path</u>
Book 1: <u>A Taste for a Mate</u>
Book 2: <u>Trinity Bound</u>
Book 2.5: <u>A Night Away</u>
Book 3: <u>Enforcer's Redemption</u>
Book 3.5: <u>Blurred Expectations</u>

Book 3.7: <u>Forgiveness</u>
Book 4: <u>Shattered Emotions</u>
Book 5: <u>Hidden Destiny</u>
Book 5.5: <u>A Beta's Haven</u>
Book 6: <u>Fighting Fate</u>
Book 6.5: <u>Loving the Omega</u>
Book 6.7: <u>The Hunted Heart</u>
Book 7: <u>Wicked Wolf</u>

The Elements of Five Series:
Book 1: From Breath and Ruin
Book 2: From Flame and Ash
Book 3: From Spirit and Binding
Book 4: From Shadow and Silence

Dante's Circle Series:
Book 1: <u>Dust of My Wings</u>
Book 2: <u>Her Warriors' Three Wishes</u>
Book 3: <u>An Unlucky Moon</u>
Book 3.5: <u>His Choice</u>
Book 4: <u>Tangled Innocence</u>
Book 5: <u>Fierce Enchantment</u>
Book 6: <u>An Immortal's Song</u>
Book 7: <u>Prowled Darkness</u>
Book 8: Dante's Circle Reborn

Holiday, Montana Series:
>Book 1: <u>Charmed Spirits</u>
>Book 2: <u>Santa's Executive</u>
>Book 3: <u>Finding Abigail</u>
>Book 4: <u>Her Lucky Love</u>
>Book 5: Dreams of Ivory

The Branded Pack Series:
(Written with Alexandra Ivy)
>Book 1: <u>Stolen and Forgiven</u>
>Book 2: <u>Abandoned and Unseen</u>
>Book 3: <u>Buried and Shadowed</u>

From the Forever Rule
Aston

> The Cages are the most presti-
> gious family in Denver—at least
> according to the patriarch of the
> Cage family.
> And the Cages have rules.
> Rules only they know.

I always knew that one day my father would die. I hadn't realized that day would come so soon. Or that the last words I would say to him would've been in anger.

I had been having one of the best nights of my life, a beautiful woman in my arms, and a smile on my face when I received the phone call that had changed my family's life.

The fact that I had been smiling had been a shock, because according to my brothers, I didn't smile much. I was far too busy being *The Cage* of Cage Enterprises.

We were a dominant force in the city of Denver when it came to certain real estate ventures, as well as being one of the only ethical and environmentally friendly ones who tried to keep up with that. We had our hands in countless different pots around the world, but mostly we gravitated in the state of Colorado—our home.

I had not created the company, no, that honor had gone to my grandfather, and then my father. The Cage Enterprises were and would always be a family endeavor. And when my father had stepped away a few years ago, stating he had wanted to see the world, and also see if his sons could actually take up the mantle, I had stepped in—not that the man believed we could.

My brothers were in various roles within the company, at least those who had wanted to be part of it. But I was the face of Cage Enterprises.

So no, I hadn't smiled often. There wasn't time.

We weren't billionaires with mega yachts. We worked seventy-hour weeks to make sure *all* our employees had a livable wage while wining and dining with those who looked down at us for not being on their level. And others thought we were the high and mighty anyway since they didn't understand us. So, I didn't smile.

But I had smiled that night.

It had been a gala for some charity, one I couldn't even remember off the top of my head. We had donated between the company and my own finances—we always did. But I couldn't even remember anything about why we were there.

Yet I could remember her smile. The heat in her eyes when she had looked up at me, the feel of her body pressed against mine as we had danced along the dance floor, and then when we ended up in the hallway, bodies pressed against one another, needing each other, wanting each other.

And I had put aside all my usual concepts of business and life to have this woman in my arms.

And then my mother had called and had shattered that illusion.

"Your father is dead."

She hadn't even braced me for the blow. A heart

attack on a vacation on a beach in Majorca, and he was dead. She hadn't cried, hadn't said anything, just told me that I had to be the one to tell my brothers.

And so, I had, all six of them. Because of course Loren Cage would have seven sons. He couldn't do things just once, he had to make sure he left his legacy, his destiny.

And that was why we were here today, in a high-rise in Centennial, waiting on my father's lawyer to show up with the reading of the will.

"Hey, when is Winstone going to get here?" Dorian asked, his typical high energy playing on his face, and how he tapped his fingers along the hand-carved wooden table.

I stared at my brother, at those piercing blue eyes that matched my own, and frowned. He should be here soon. He did call us all here after all."

"I still don't know why we all had to be here for the reading of the will," Hudson whispered as he stared off into the distance. Neither Dorian nor Hudson worked for Cage Enterprises. They had stock with the company, and a few other connections because that's what family did, but they didn't work on the same floors as some of us and hadn't been elbow to elbow with our father before he had retired. Though dear old dad had worked in our small town more often than not in the end. In fact, Hudson didn't even live in Denver anymore. He had moved to the town we owned in the mountains.

Because of course we Cages owned a damned town. Part of me wasn't sure if the concept of having our name on everything within the town had been on purpose or had occurred organically. Though knowing my grandfather, perhaps it had been exactly what he'd wanted. He had bought up a few buildings, built a few more, and now we owned three-quarters of the town, including the major resort which brought in tourists and income.

And that was why we were here.

"You have to be here because you're evidently in the will," I said softly, trying not to get annoyed that we were waiting for our father's lawyer. Again.

"You would think he would be able to just send us a memo. I mean, it should be clear right? We all know what stakes we have in, we should just be able to do things evenly," Theo said, his gaze off into the distance. My younger brother also didn't work for the company, instead he had decided to go to culinary school, something my father had hated. But you couldn't control a Cage, that was sort of our deal.

"Why would you be cut out of the will?" I asked, honestly curious.

"Because I married a man and a woman," he drawled out. "You know he hasn't spoken to me since before the wedding," Ford said, and I saw the hurt in his gaze even though I knew he was probably trying to hide it.

"Well, he was an asshole, what do you expect?" James asked.

I looked behind Ford to see my brother and co-chair of Cage Enterprises standing with his hands in his pockets, staring out the window.

With Flynn, our vice president, standing beside him, they looked like the heads of businesses they were. While they wore suits and so did I, we were the only ones.

Dorian and Hudson were both in jeans, Hudson's having a hole at the knee. And probably not as a fashion statement, most likely because it had torn at some point, and he hadn't bothered to buy another pair. Theo was in slacks, but a Henley with his sleeves pushed up, tapping his finger just like Hudson, clearly wanting to get out of here as well. Ford had on cargo pants, and a tight black T-shirt, and looked like he had just gotten off his shift. He owned a security company with his husband and a few other friends, and did security for the Cages when he could, though I knew he didn't like to work with family often. And I knew it wasn't because of us. No, it was Father—even if he had officially *retired*. It was always Father.

And he was gone.

"Can't believe the asshole's gone," I whispered.

Ford's brows rose. "Look at that, you calling him an asshole. I'm proud."

"You should show him respect," Mother said as she came inside the room, her high heels tapping against the marble floors. I didn't bother standing up like I normally would have, because Melanie Cage looked to be in a *mood*.

She didn't look sad that Dad was gone, more like angry that he would dare go against their plans. What plans? I didn't know, but that was my mother.

She came right up to Dorian and leaned down to kiss his cheek. She didn't even bother to look at the rest of us. Dorian was Mother's favorite. Which I knew Dorian resented, but I didn't have to deal with mommy issues at this moment.

No, we had to deal with father issues at this point.

"I'm going to go get him," Flynn replied, turning toward the door. "I'm really not in the mood to wait any longer, especially since he's being so secretive about this meeting."

As I had been thinking just the same, I nodded at Flynn though he didn't need my permission. However, just then, the door opened, and I frowned when it wasn't just Mr. Winstone walking into the conference room.

I stared as an older woman walked through the door following Mr. Winstone, and four women and another man with messy hair and tattered cut-up jeans that matched Hudson's walked behind them.

The guy looked familiar, as if I'd seen him somewhere, or maybe it was just his eyes.

Where had I seen those eyes before?

"Phoebe? What are you doing here?" Ford asked as he moved forward and gripped the hands of one of the women.

"I was going to ask the same question," Phoebe asked as she looked at Ford, then around the room.

Those of us sitting stood up, confused about why this other family—because they were clearly a family—had decided to enter the room.

"We're here to meet the lawyer about my father's death, Ford. Why would you and the Cages be here?" she asked, and I wondered how the hell Mr. Winstone had fucked up so badly? Why the hell was he letting another family that clearly seemed to be in shock come into our room? This wasn't how he normally handled things.

Ford was the one who answered though—thankfully—because I had no idea what the hell was going on.

"Phoebe, we're here for my dad's will reading. What the hell is going on?" he asked. Phoebe looked around, as well as the others.

I stared at them, at the tall willowy one with wide eyes, at the smaller one with tears still in her eyes as if she was the only one truly mourning, and at the woman who seemed to be in charge, not the mother. Instead she had shrewd eyes and was glaring at all of us. The man stood back, hands in pockets, and looked just as shell-shocked as Ford.

But before Mr. Winstone or anyone else could say anything, my mother spoke in such a crisp, icy tone that I froze.

"I don't know why you're acting so dramatic. You knew your father was an asshole. He just liked creating drama," she snapped.

As I tried to catch up with her words, the older woman answered. "Melanie, stop."

This couldn't be happening. Because things started to click into place. The fact that the man at the other end of this table had our eyes, and that everybody looked so fucking shocked. I didn't know how Ford knew this Phoebe, and I would be getting answers.

"We had a deal," my mother continued, as it seemed that the rest of us were just now catching on. "You would keep your family away from mine. We would share Loren, but I got the name, I got the family. You got whatever else. But now it looks like Loren decided to be an asshole again."

"What are you talking about?" the shrewd sister asked as she came forward, her hands fisted at her side.

"Excuse me," I said, clearing my throat. I was going to be damned if I let anyone else handle this meeting. I was The Cage now. "Will someone please explain?"

"Well, I wasn't quite sure how this was going to work out," Mr. Winstone began, and we all quieted, while I wanted to strangle the man. What did he mean how *the hell this would work out*? What was this?

This seemed like a big fucking mistake.

"Loren Cage had certain provisions in his will for both of his families. And one of the many requirements that I will go over today is that this meeting must take place." He paused and I hoped it wasn't for effect, because I was going to throttle him if it was. "Loren Cage had two families. Seven sons with his wife Melanie, and four daughters and a son with his mistress, Constance."

"We went by partner," the other mother corrected.

I blinked, counting the adults in the room. "Twelve?" I asked, my voice slightly high-pitched.

"Busy fucking man," Dorian whispered.

Hudson snorted, while we just stood and stared at each other.

This could not be happening. A secret family? No, we were not that cliché.

"I can't do this," Phoebe blurted, her eyes wide.

"Oh, stop overreacting," my mother scorned.

"Do not talk to my daughter that way." The other mother glared.

"It was always going to be an issue," Mother continued. "All the secrets and the lies. And now the kids will have to deal with it. Because God forbid Loren ever deal with anything other than his own dick."

"That's enough," I snapped.

"Don't you dare talk to us like that," the shrewd sister snapped right back.

"I will talk however I damn well please. I am going to need to know exactly how this happened," I shouted over everyone else's words.

Out of the corner of my eye I saw Phoebe run through the door. Ford followed and then the tall willowy one joined.

"Shit," I snapped.

"Language," Mother bit out.

I laughed. "Really? You are going to talk to me about language."

I looked over at James, who shrugged, before he put two fingers in his mouth and whistled that high-pitched whistle that only he could do.

Everyone froze as Theo rubbed his ear and glared at me.

"Winstone," I said through gritted teeth. "I take it we all have to be here in order for this to happen?"

He cleared his throat. "At least a majority. But you all had to at least step into the room."

"Excuse me then," I said.

"You're just going to leave? Just like that?" my mother asked.

I whirled on her. "I'm going to go see if my

apparent *family* is okay. Then I'm going to come back and we're going to get answers. Because there is no way that I'm going to leave here without them."

I stormed out the door, and thankfully nobody followed me.

Of course, though, I shouldn't have been too swift with that, as the woman who had to be the eldest sister practically ran to my side, her heels tapping against the marble.

"I'm coming with you."

"That's just fine." I paused, knowing that I wasn't angry at these people. No, my father and apparently our mothers were the ones that had to deal with this. I looked over at the woman who Mr. Winstone and the mothers had claimed was my sister and cleared my throat.

"I'm Aston."

"Is this really the time for introductions?" she asked.

"I'm about to go see your sister and my brother to make sure that they're fine, so sure. I would like to know the name of the woman that is running next to me right now."

"I'm running, you're walking quickly because you have such long legs."

I snorted, surprised I could even do that.

"I'm Isabella," she replied after a moment.

"I would say nice to meet you Isabella…" I let my voice trail off.

She let out a sharp laugh before shaking her head. "I'm going to need a moment to wrap my head around this, but not now."

"Same."

We stormed out of the building, and I lagged behind since Ford was standing in front of Phoebe who was in the arms of another man with dark hair and everybody seemed to be talking all at once.

"I just. I can't deal with this right now," Phoebe said, and I realized that something else must have been going on with her right then. She looked tired, and far more emotional than the rest of us.

I looked over at the man holding her and blinked. "Kane?" I asked.

Kane stared at me and let out a breath. "Wow," he said with a laugh.

"We'll handle it," Isabella put in, completely ignoring us. "And if we need to meet again later, we will." Then she looked over at Ford and I, with such menace in her gaze, I nearly took a step back. "Is that a problem?"

I raised my chin, glaring right back at her. "Not

at all. However I want answers, so I'd rather not have the meeting canceled right now. But I'm also not going to force any of my," I paused, realization hitting far too hard, *"family* to stay if they don't want to."

And with that, I turned on my heel and went back into the building, with Isabella and Ford following me. Everyone was still yelling in the interim, and I cleared my throat. As Isabella had done it at the same time, everyone paused to look at me.

"Read the damn will. Because we need answers," I ordered Winstone, and he shook like a leaf before nodding.

"Okay. We can do that." He cleared his throat, then he began going over trusts and incomes and buildings and things that I would care about soon, but what I wanted to know was what the hell our father had been thinking about.

"Here's the tricky part," Winstone began, as we all leaned forward, eager to hear what the hell he had to say.

"The family money, not of the business, not of each of your inheritance from other family members, but the bulk of Loren Cage's assets will be split between all twelve kids."

"Are you kidding me?" Isabella asked. "What money? We weren't exactly poor, but we were solidly middle class."

"We did just fine," the other mother pleaded.

My mother snorted, clearly not believing the words.

I glared at the woman who raised me, willing her to say *anything*. She would probably be pushed out of the window at that point. Not by me, by someone else, but she probably would've earned it.

The lawyer continued. "However to retain the majority of current assets and to keep Cage Lake and all of its subsidiaries you will have to meet as a family once a month for three years. If this does not happen, Cage Enterprises will be broken into multiple parts and sold." He went on into the legalese that I ignored as I tried to hear over the blood pounding in my ears.

"You own a town?" the other man asked.

I looked over at the one man in the room I didn't know the name of. "Not exactly."

"Kyler," Isabella whispered.

In that moment, I realized that I had a brother named Kyler—if this was all to be believed.

"This can't be legal right?" the tall willowy person said.

"Yes Sophia, it can," their mother put in.

Oh good, another sister named Sophia.

Only one name to go. What the hell was wrong with me?

I forced my jaw to relax. "Are you telling us that we need to have all twelve of us at dinner once a month for three years in order to keep what is rightly inherited to us? To keep people in business and keep their jobs?"

"We don't need the money, but everyone else in our employ does," James snapped. "As do those we work with."

"Damn straight," Dorian growled.

"How are we supposed to believe this?" I asked, asking the obvious question.

"First, only five must attend, and two must be of a different family." The lawyer continued as if I hadn't spoken. "Of course you are *all* family…"

"Again, how are we supposed to believe this?" I asked.

"Here are the DNA tests already done."

"Are you fucking kidding me?" Isabella asked.

I looked at her, as she had literally taken the words out of my mouth.

"Isn't that sort of like a violation?" Kyler asked, his face pale.

"We need to get our own lawyers on this," James whispered.

I nodded tightly, knowing we had much more to say on this.

"There's no way this is legal," the youngest said, and I looked over at her.

"What's your name?" I asked.

"Emily. Emily Cage Dixon," she said softly, and we all froze.

"Your middle name is Cage?" I asked, biting out the words.

"All of our middle names are Cage," Sophia said, shaking her head. "I hated it but Dad wanted to be cute because our father's name was Cage Dixon, or maybe it wasn't. Is he also a bigamist?" she asked.

Her mother lifted her chin. "We never married. And no, your father's name was not Dixon, that was my maiden name."

"What?" Sophia asked. "All this time…are our grandparents even dead?"

"Yes, my parents are dead. The same with Loren's." The other mother's eyes filled with tears. "I'm sorry we lied."

"We'll get to that later," Isabella put in, and I was grateful.

I let out a breath. "In order to keep our assets, in

order to keep the family name intact, we need to have *dinner*. For three years."

The small lawyer nodded, his glasses falling down his nose. "At least five of you. And it can start three months after the funeral, which we can plan after this."

"This is ridiculous," Hudson murmured under his breath, before he got up and walked out.

I watched him go, knowing he had his own demons, and tried to understand what the hell was going on. "Why did he do this?" I asked, more to myself than anyone else.

"I never really knew the man, but apparently none of us did," Isabella said, staring off into the distance.

"Leave the paperwork and go," I ordered Winstone, and he didn't even mutter a peep. Instead, he practically ran out of the room. James and Flynn immediately went to the paperwork, and I knew they were scouring it. But from the way that their jaws tightened, I had a feeling that my father had found a way to make this legal. Because we would always have a choice to lose everything. That was the man.

"It's true," my mother put in. "You all share the same father. That was the deal when we got married, and when he decided to bring this other woman into our lives."

"I'm pretty sure you were the other woman," the other mom said.

I pinched the bridge of my nose.

"Stop. All of you." I stared at the group and realized that I was probably the eldest Cage here, other than the moms. I would deal with this. We didn't have a choice. "Whatever happens, we'll deal with it."

"You're in charge now?" Isabella asked, but Sophia shushed her.

I was grateful for that, because I had a feeling Isabella and I were going to butt heads more often than not.

I shrugged, trying to act as if my world hadn't been rocked. "I would say welcome to the Cages, because DNA evidence seems to point that way, however perhaps you were already one of us all along."

Kyler muttered something under his breath I couldn't hear before speaking up. "You have my eyes," he said.

I nodded. "Noticed that too."

The other man tilted his head. "So what, we do dinners and we make nice?"

I sighed. "We don't have to be adversaries."

"You say that as if you're the one in charge," Isabella said again.

"Because he is," Theo said, and they all stared at him.

I tried to tamp down the pride swelling at those words—along with the overwhelming pressure.

Theo continued. "He's the eldest. He's the one that takes care of us. And he's the CEO of Cage Enterprises. He's going to be the one that deals with the paperwork fallout."

"Because family is just paperwork?" Emily asked, her voice lost.

I shook my head. "No, family is insane, and apparently, it's been secret all along. And it looks like we have a few introductions to make, and a few tests to redo. But if it turns out it's true, we're Cages, and we don't back down."

"And what does that mean?" Isabella asked, her tone far too careful.

Theo was the one who finally answered. "It means we're going to have to figure shit out."

And for just an instant, the thought of that beautiful woman with that gorgeous smile came to mind, and I pushed those thoughts away. My family was breaking, or perhaps breaking open. And I didn't have time to worry about things like a woman who had made me smile.

The Cages needed me and after today's meeting there would be no going back to sanity.

Ever.

In the mood to read another family saga? Meet the Cage Family in The Forever Rule!

From One Way Back to Me
Eli

When my morning begins with me standing ankle-deep in a basement full of water, I know I probably should have stayed in bed. Only, I was the boss, and I didn't get that choice.

"Hold on. I'm looking for it." East cursed underneath his breath as my younger brother bent down around the pipe, trying his best to turn off the valve. I sighed, waded through the muck in my work boots, and moved to help him. "I said I've got it," East snapped, but I ignored him.

I narrowed my eyes at the evil pipe. "It's old and rusted, and even though it passed an inspection over a year ago, we knew this was going to be a problem."

"And I'm the fucking handyman of this company. I've got this."

"And as a handyman, you need a hand."

"You're hilarious. Seriously. I don't know how I could ever manage without your wit and humor." The dryness in his tone made my lips twitch even as I did my best to ignore the smell of whatever water we stood in.

"Fuck you," I growled.

"No thanks. I'm a little too busy for that."

With a grunt, East shut off the water, and we both stood back, hands on our hips as we stared at the mess of this basement.

East let out a sigh. "I'm not going to have to turn the water off for the whole property, but I'm glad that we don't have tenants in this particular cabin."

I nodded tightly and held back a sigh. "This is probably why there aren't basements in Texas. Because everything seems to go wrong in these things."

"I'm pretty sure this is a storm shelter, or at least a tornado one. Not quite sure as it's one of the only basements in the area."

"It was probably the only one that they had the energy to make back in the day. Considering this whole place is built over clay and limestone."

East nodded, looked around. "I'll start the cleanup with this water, and we'll look to see what we can do with the pipes."

I pinched the bridge of my nose. "I don't want to have to replace the plumbing for this whole place."

"At least it's not the villa itself, or the farmhouse, or the winery. Just a single cabin."

I glared at my younger brother, then reached out and knocked on a wooden pillar. "Shut your mouth. Don't say things like that to me. We are just now getting our feet under us."

East shrugged. "It's the truth, though. However much you weigh it, it could have been worse."

I pinched the bridge of my nose. "Jesus Christ. You were in the military for how long? A Wilder your entire life, and you say things like that? When the hell did you lose that superstition bone?"

"About the time that my Humvee was blown up, and when Evan's was, Everett's too. Hell, about the time that you almost fell out of the sky in your plane. Or when Elliot was nearly shot to death trying to help one of his men. So, yes, I pretty much lost all superstition when trying to toe the line ended up in near death and maiming."

I met my brother's gaze, that familiar pang

thinking about all that we had lost and almost lost over the past few years.

East muttered under his breath, shaking his head. "And I sound more and more like Evan these days rather than myself."

I squeezed his shoulder and let out a breath, thinking of our brother who grunted more than spoke these days. "It's okay. We've been through a lot. But we're here."

Somehow, we were here. I wasn't quite sure if we had made the right decision about two years ago when we had formed this plan, or rather *I* had formed this plan, but there was no going back. We were in it, and we were going to have to find a way to make it work, flooded former tornado shelters and all.

East sighed. "I'll work on this now. Then I'll head on over to the main house. I have a few things to work on there."

"You know, we can hire you help. I know we had all the contractors and everything to work with us for some of the rebuilds and rehabs, but we can hire someone else for you on a day-to-day basis."

My brother shook his head. "We may be able to afford it, but I'd rather save that for a rainy day. Because when it rains, it pours here, and flash flooding is a major threat in this part of Texas." He winked as he said it, mixing his metaphors, and I just shook my head.

"You just let me know if you need it."

"You're the CEO, brother of mine, not the CFO. That's Everett."

"True, but we did talk about it so we can work on it." I paused, thinking about what other expenses might show up. "And what do you need to do with the villa?"

The villa was the main house where most things happened on the property. It contained the lobby, library, and atrium. My apartment was also on the top floor, so I could be there for emergencies. Our innkeeper lived on the other side of the house, but I was in the main loft because this was my project, my baby.

My other brothers, all five of them, lived in cabins on the property. We lived together, worked together, ate together, and fought together. We were the Wilder brothers. It was what we did.

I had left to join the Air Force at seventeen, having graduated early, leaving behind my kid brothers and sister. After nearly twenty years of doing what we needed to in order to survive, we hadn't spent as much time with one another as I would have liked. We hadn't been stationed together, so we hadn't seen one another for longer than holidays or in passing.

But now we were together. At least most of us. So I was going to make this work, even if it killed me.

East finally answered my question. "I just have to fix a door that's a little too squeaky in one of the guestrooms. Not a big deal."

I raised a brow. "That's it?"

"It's one of the many things on my list. Thankfully, this place is big enough that I always have something to do. It's an unending list. And that the winery has its own team to work on all of that shit, because I'm not in the mood to learn to deal with any of the complicated machinery that comes with that world."

I snorted. "Honestly, same. I'm glad there are people that know what the fuck they're doing when it comes to wine making so that didn't have to be the two of us."

I left my brother to this job, knowing he liked time on his own, just like the rest of us did, and went to dry my boots. I was working by myself for most of the day, in interviews and other "boss business," as Elliot called it, so I had to focus and get clean.

I wasn't in the mood to deal with interviews, but it was part of my job. We had to fill positions that hadn't been working out over the past year, some more than others.

Wilder Retreat was a place that hadn't been even a spark in my mind my entire life. No, I had been too busy being a career military man—getting in my twenty, moving up the ranks, and ending up as a Lieutenant Colonel before I got out. I had been a commander of a squadron, and yet, it felt like I didn't know how to command where I was now.

When my sister Eliza had lost her husband when he was on deployment, it had been the last domino to fall in the Wilder brothers' military career. I had been ready to get out with twenty years in, knowing I needed a career outside of being a Lieutenant Colonel. I wasn't even forty yet, and the term retirement was a misnomer, but that's what happened when it came to my former job.

East had been getting out around that time for reasons of his own, and then Evan had been forced to. I rubbed my hand over my chest, that familiar pain, remembering the phone call from one of Evan's commanders when Evan had been hurt.

I thought I'd lost my baby brother then, and we nearly had. Everett had gotten hurt too, and Elijah and Elliot had needed out for their own reasons. Losing our baby sister's husband had just pushed us forward.

Finding out that Eliza's husband had been a cheating asshole had just cemented the fact that we needed to spend more time together as a family so we could be there for one another.

In retrospect, it would have been nice if Eliza would have been able to come down to Texas with us, to our suburb outside of San Antonio. Only, she had fallen in love again, with a man with a big family and a good heart up in Fort Collins, Colorado. She was still up there and traveled down enough that we actually got to get to know our sister again.

It was weird to think that, after so many years of always seeing each other in passing or through video calls, most of us were here, opening up a business. And all because I had been losing my mind.

Wilder Retreat and Winery was a villa and wedding venue outside of San Antonio. We were in hill country, at least what passed for hill country in South Texas, and the place had been owned by a former Air Force General who had wanted to retire and sell the place, since his kid didn't want it.

It was a large spread that used to be a ranch back in the day, nearly one hundred acres that the original owners had taken from a working ranch, and instead of making it a dude ranch or something similar, like others did around here, they'd added a winery using local help. We were close enough to Fredericksburg that it made sense in terms of the soil and weather. They had been able to add on additions, so it wasn't just the winery. Someone could come for the day for a winery tour or even a retreat tour, but most people came for the weekend or for a whole week. There were cabins and a farmhouse where we held weddings, dances, or other events. We had some chickens and ducks that gave us eggs, and goats that seemed to have a mind of their own and provided milk for cheese. Then there was the main annex, which housed all the equipment for the retreat villa.

The winery had its own section of buildings, and it was far bigger than anything I would have ever thought that we could handle. But, between the six of us, we did.

And the only reason we could even afford it, because one didn't afford something like this on a military salary, even with a decent retirement plan, was because of our uncles.

Our uncles, Edward and Edmond Wilder, had owned Wilder Wines down in Napa, California, for years. They had done well for themselves, and when we had been kids, we had gone out to visit. Evan had been the one that had clung to it and had been interested in wine making before he had changed his mind and gone into the military like the rest of us.

That was why Evan was in charge of the winery itself now. Because he knew what he was doing, even if he'd growled and said he didn't. Either way though, the place was huge, had multiple working parts at all times, and we had a staff that needed us. But when the uncles had died, they had left the money from the sale of the winery to us in equal parts. Eliza had taken hers to invest for her future children, and the rest of us had pooled our money together to buy this place and make it ours. A lot of the staff from the old owner had stayed, but some had left as well. Because they didn't want new owners who had no idea what they were doing, or they just retired. Either way, we were over a year in and doing okay.

Except for two positions that made me want to groan.

I had an interview with who would be our third wedding planner since we started this. The main component of the retreat was to have an actual wedding venue. To be able to host parties, and not just wine tours. Elliot was our major event planner that helped with our yearly and seasonal minute details, but he didn't want anything to do with the actual weddings. That was a whole other skill set, and so we wanted a wedding planner. We had gone through two wedding planners now, and we needed to hire a third. The first one had lied on her résumé, had given references that were her friends who had lied and had even created websites that were all fabrication, all so she could get into the business. Which, I understood, getting into the business is one thing. However, lying was another. Plus, we needed someone with actual experience because we didn't have any ourselves. We were going out on a limb here with this whole retreat business, and it was all because I had the harebrained idea of getting our family to work together, get along, and get to know one another. I wanted us to have a future, to be our own bosses.

And it was so far over my head that I knew that if I didn't get reliable help, we were going to fail.

Later, I had a meeting with that potential

wedding planner. But first, I had to see what the fuck that smell was coming from the main kitchen in the villa.

The second wedding planner we hired was a guy with great and *true* references, one who was good at his job but hated everything to do with my brothers and me. He had hated the idea of the retreat and how rustic it was, even though we were in fucking South Texas. Yes, the buildings look slightly European because that was the theme that the original owners had gone for. Still, the guy had hated us, hadn't listened to us, and had called us white trash before he had walked away, jumped into his convertible, and sped off down the road, leaving us without help. He had been rude to our guests, and now Elliot was the one having to plan weddings for the past three weeks. My brother was going to strangle me soon if we didn't hire someone. And this person was going to be our last hope. As soon as she showed up, that was.

I looked down on my watch and tried to plan the rest of my day. I had thirty minutes to figure out what the hell was going on in the kitchen, and then I had to go to the meeting.

I nodded at a few guests who were sipping wine and eating a cheese plate and then at our innkeeper,

Naomi. Naomi's honey-brown hair was cut in an angled bob that lit her face, and she grinned at me.

"Hello there, Boss Man," she whispered. "You might need to go to the kitchen."

"Do I want to know?" I asked with a grumble.

"I'm not sure. But I am going to go check in our next guest, and then Elliott needs to meet with the Henderson couple."

"He'll be there." I didn't say that Elliot would rather chew off his own arm rather than deal with this, considering we had a family event coming in, one that Elliot was on target with planning. The wedding for next year was an important one, so we needed to work on it.

Naomi was a fantastic innkeeper, far more organized than any of us—and that was saying something since my brothers and I knew our way around schedules, to-do lists, and spreadsheets. Naomi was personable, smiled, and kept us on our toes.

Without her, I knew we wouldn't be able to do this. Hell, without Amos, our vineyard manager, I knew that Evan and Elijah wouldn't be able to handle the winery as they did. Naomi and Amos had come with the place when we had bought it, and I would be forever grateful that they had decided to stay on.

I gave Naomi another nod, then headed back to the kitchen and nearly walked right back out.

Tony stood there, a scowl on his face and his hands on his hips. "I don't understand what the fuck is wrong with this oven."

"What's going on?" I asked as Everett stood by Tony. Everett was my quiet brother with usually a small smile on his face, only right then it looked like he was ready to scream.

I didn't know why Everett was even there since he was part responsible for the financials side of the company and usually worked with Elliot these days. Maybe he had come to the kitchen after the smell of burning as I had after Naomi's prodding.

Tony threw his hands in the air. "What's going on? This stove is a piece of shit. All of it is a piece of shit. I'm tired of this rustic place. I thought I would be coming to a Michelin star restaurant. To be my own chef. Instead, I have to make English breakfasts and pancakes with bananas. I might as well be at a bed and breakfast."

I pinched the bridge of my nose. "We're an inn, not a bed and breakfast."

"But I serve breakfast. That's all I do these days. That and cheese platters. Nobody comes for dinner. Nobody comes for lunch."

That was a lie. Tony worked for the winery and the retreat itself and served all the meals. But Tony wanted to go crazy with the menu, to try new and fantastical items that just weren't going to work here.

And I had a feeling I was going to throw up if I wasn't careful.

"I quit," Tony snapped, and I knew right then, it was done for. I was done.

"You can't quit," I growled while Everett held back a sigh.

"Yes, I can. I'm done. I'm done with you and this ranch. You're not cowboys. You're not even Texans. You're just people moving in on our territory." And with that, Tony stomped away, throwing his chef's apron on the ground.

I was thankful that the kitchen was on the other side of the library and front area, where most of the guests were if they weren't out on one of the tours of the area and city that Elliott had arranged for them. That was the whole point of this retreat. They could come visit, and could relax, or we could set them up on a tour of downtown San Antonio, or Canyon Lake, or any of the other places that were nearby.

And yet, Tony had just thrown a wrench into all of that. I didn't know what was worse, the smell of burning, Tony leaving, the water in the basement that wasn't truly a basement, or the fact that I was going to smell like charred food and wet jeans when I went to go meet this wedding planner.

"You're going to need to hire a new cook," Everett whispered.

I looked at my brother, at the man who did his best to make sure we didn't go bankrupt, and I wanted to just grumble. "I figured."

"I can help for now, but you know I'm only part-time. I can't stay away from my twins for too long," Sandy said as she came forward to take the pan off the stove. "I wish I could do full time, but this is all I can do for now."

Sandy had come back from maternity leave after we had already opened the retreat. She had been on with the former owners and was brilliant. But she had a right to be a mom and not want to work full time. I understood that, and I knew that Sandy didn't want to handle a whole kitchen by herself. She liked her position as a sous chef.

I was going to have to figure out what to do. Again.

"I'll get it done," I said while rubbing my temples.

"You know what we need to do," Everett whispered, and I shook my head.

"He'll kill us."

"Maybe, but it'll be worth it in the end. And speaking of, don't you have that interview soon? Or do you want me to take it?" His gaze tracked to my jeans.

I shook my head. "No, help Sandy."

Everett winced. "Just because I know how to slice an onion, it doesn't mean I'm good at cooking."

"I'm sorry, did you just say you could slice an onion? Get to it," Sandy put in with a smile, pointing at the sink. "Wash those hands."

"I cannot believe I just said that out loud. I just stepped right into it," Everett said with a sigh. "Go to the interview. You know what to ask."

"I do. And I hope we don't get screwed this time."

"You know, if we're lucky, we'll get someone as good as Roy's wedding planner, or at least that woman that we met. You know who she is." Everett grinned like a cat with the canary.

I narrowed my eyes. "Don't bring her up."

"Oh, I can't help it. A single dance, and you were drawn to her."

"What dance? You know what? No, I don't have

time. We have to work on lunch and dinner. Tell me while you work," Sandy added with a wink.

Everett leaned toward her as he washed his hands. "Well, you see, there was this dance, and he met the perfect woman, and then she got engaged."

Sandy's eyes widened. "Engaged? How did that happen? She was dating someone else?" she asked as she looked at me.

I pinched the bridge of my nose. "It was at Roy's place when we were looking at the venue to see if we wanted to buy the retreat here." I sighed, I knew if I just let it all out, she would move on from this conversation, and I would never have to deal with it again. "Somehow, I ended up at a wedding there, caught the garter. This woman caught the bouquet, and she happened to be the wedding planner. We danced, we laughed, and as she walked away, her boyfriend got down on one knee and proposed."

"No way!" She leaned forward with a fierce look on her face, her eyes bright. "What did she say?"

"I have no clue. I left." I ignored whatever feeling might want to show up at that thought. Everett gave me a glance, and I shook my head. "Enough of that. Yes, the wedding that she did was great, but I honestly have no idea who she is, and she has a job. She doesn't need to work here." And I didn't know what I would do if I saw her again or had to work with her. There had been such an intense connection that I knew it would be awkward as hell. But thankfully, she had her own business and wasn't going to come to the Wilder Retreat for a job.

I left Sandy and Everett on their own, knowing that they were capable, at least for now. And I knew who we would have to hire if she said yes, and if my other brother didn't kill me first.

I washed my hands in the sink on the way out, grateful that at least I looked somewhat decent, if not a little disheveled, and made my way out front, hoping that the wedding planner who came in through the doors would be the one that would stick. Because we needed some good luck. After the day we've had, we needed some good luck.

I turned the corner and nearly tripped over my feet.

Because, of course, fate was this way.

It was her.

Of all the wedding planners from all the wedding venues, it was her.

In the mood to read another family saga? Meet the Wilder Brothers in One Way Back to Me!

FROM BITTERSWEET PROMISES
LEIF

"Not only did you convince me to somehow go on a blind date, it became a double date. How on earth did you work this magic on me, cousin?" I asked Lake as she leaned against the pillar just inside the restaurant.

Lake grinned at me, her dark hair pulled away from her face. She had on this swingy black dress and looked as if she were excited, anxious, nervous, and happy all at the same time. Considering she was bouncing on her toes when usually Lake was calm, cool, and collected, was saying something. "I asked, and you said yes. Because you love me."

"I might love you because we're family, but I still think we're making a mistake." I shook my head and pulled at my shirt sleeves. Lake had somehow convinced me to wear a button-up shirt tucked into gray pants, I even had on shiny shoes. I looked like a damn banker. But if that's what Lake wanted, that's what I would do.

Lake might technically be my cousin, even though we weren't blood-related, but we were more like brother and sister than any of my other cousins.

I had siblings, as did Lake, but with the generational gap, we were at least a decade older than all of our other cousins. That meant, despite the fact that we had lived over an hour apart for most of our lives, we'd grown up more like siblings.

I loved my three younger siblings and talked to them daily. Unlike some blended families, they *were* my brothers and sister and not like strangers or distant family members. I didn't feel a disconnect from the three of them, but Lake was still closer to me.

Probably because we were either heading into our thirties or already there, where most of our other cousins were either just now in their early twenties or still teenagers in high school. With how big we Montgomerys were as a family, it made sense that there would be such a widespread age group. That meant that Lake and I were best friends, cousins, practically siblings, and sometimes the banes of each other's existences.

We were also business owners and partners and saw each other too often these days. That was probably why she convinced me to go on a blind double date. But she had been out with Zach before. I, however, had never met May. Lake had some connection with her that I wasn't sure about, and for some reason Lake's date had said yes to this double date.

And, in the complicated way of family, I had agreed to it. I must have been tired. Or perhaps I'd had too many beers. Because I didn't do blind dates, and recently, I didn't do dates at all.

Lake scanned her phone, then looked up at me, all innocence in her smart gaze. "You shouldn't have told me you wanted to settle down in your old age."

I narrowed my eyes. "I'm still in my early thirties, jerk. Stop calling me old."

"I shouldn't call you old since you're only a few years older than me." She fluttered her eyelashes and I flipped her off, ignoring the stare from the older woman next to me. Though I was a tattoo artist, I didn't have many visible tattoos. Most of mine were on my back and legs, hidden from the world unless I wanted to show them. I hadn't figured out what I wanted on my arms beyond a few small pieces on my wrists and upper shoulders. And since tattoos were permanent, I was taking my time. If a client needed to see my skin with ink to feel comfortable, I'd show them my back. My body was a canvas, so I did what I could to set people at ease.

But I still had the eyebrow piercing and had recently taken out my nose ring. I didn't look too scary for most people. But apparently, flipping off a woman, growling, and cursing a time or two in front of strangers probably made me appear too close to the dark side.

"Yes, I want to settle down, but this will be awkward, won't it? Where the two of us are strangers, and the two of you aren't?" I wanted a life, a future, and yeah, one day to settle down with someone. I just didn't know why I'd mentioned it to Lake in the first place.

"If it helps, May doesn't know Zach, either. So it's a group of strangers, except I know everybody." She clapped her hands together and did her version of an evil laugh, and I just shook my head.

"Considering what you do for a living and how you like to manipulate things in your way, this makes sense. Are you going to be adding a match-making company to your conglomerate?"

Lake just fluttered her eyelashes again and laughed. Lake owned a small tech company that made a shit ton of money over the past couple of years. And because she was brilliant at what she did, innovative, and liked pushing money towards women-owned businesses, she owned more than one company at this point and was an investor in mine. I wouldn't be surprised if she found a way to open up a women-owned matchmaking company right here in town.

"It might be fun. I can call it Montgomery Links." Her eyes went wide. "Oh, my God. I have to write that down." She pulled out her phone, began to take notes, and I pinched the bridge of my nose.

"You know I trust you with my actual life, but I don't know if I trust you with my dating life."

Lake tossed her hair behind her shoulder as she continued to type. "Shut up. You love me. And once I finish setting you up, the rest of the family's next."

"Oh, really? You're going to get Daisy and Noah next?" I asked, speaking of two more of our cousins.

"Maybe. Of course, Sebastian's the only one of the younger group that seems to have a serious girlfriend."

I nodded, speaking of our other familial business partner. Sebastian was still a teenager, though in college. He had wanted to open up Montgomery Ink Legacy with me, the full title of our company. There was a legacy to it, and Sebastian had wanted in. So, though he didn't work there full-time, he was putting his future towards us. And in the ways of young love, he and his girlfriend had been together since middle school. The fact that my younger cousin was better at relationships than I was didn't make me feel great. But I was going to ignore that.

"You're not going to start up a matchmaking service, are you? Or maybe an app?"

"Dating apps are ridiculous these days, they practically want you to invest in coins to bid on dates, and that's not something I'm in the mood for. But maybe there's something I can try. I'll add it to my list."

Lake's list of inventions and tech was notorious, and knowing the brilliance of my cousin, she would one day rule the world and might eventually cross everything off that list.

"Oh, here's Zach." Lake's face brightened immediately, and she smiled up at a man with dark hair, piercing gray eyes, and an actual dimple on his cheek.

Tonight was not only about my blind date, but me getting the lay of the land when it came to Zach.

I was the first step into meeting the family. Oh, if Zach passed my gauntlet, he would meet the rest of the Montgomerys, and we were mighty. All one hundred of us.

"Zach, you're here." Lake's voice went soft, and she went on her tiptoes even in her high heels as Zach pressed a soft kiss to her lips.

"Of course, I'm here. And you're early, as usual."

Lake blushed and ducked her head. "Well, you know me. I like to be early because being on time is late," she said at the same time I did, mumbling under my breath. It was a familiar refrain when it came to us.

"Zach, good to meet you," I said, holding out my hand.

The other man gripped it firmly and shook. "Nice to meet you too, Leif. I know you might be the one on a blind date soon, but I'm nervous."

I chuckled, shaking my head. "Yeah, I'm pretty nervous too. Though I'm grateful that Lake's trying to look out for me."

My cousin laughed softly. "You totally were not saying that a few minutes ago, but be suave and sophisticated now. Or just be yourself, May's on her way."

I met Zach's gaze and we both rolled our eyes.

When I turned toward the door, I saw a woman of average height, with black straight hair, green eyes, and a sweet smile. I didn't know much about May, other than Lake knew her and liked her. If I was going to start dating again after taking time off to get the rest of my life together, I might as well start with someone that one of my best friends liked.

"May, I'm so glad that you're here," Lake said as she hugged the other woman tightly.

As Lake began to bounce on her heels, I realized that my cousin's cool, calm, and collected exterior was only for work. She was bouncing and happy when it came to her friends or when she was nervous. I knew that, of course, but I had forgotten how she had turned into the mogul that she was. It was good to see her relaxed and happy.

Now I just needed to figure out how to do that for myself.

May stood in front of me, and I felt like I was starting middle school all over again. A new school, a new life, and a past that didn't make much sense to anyone else.

I swallowed hard and nodded, not putting out my hand to shake, thinking that would be weird, but I also didn't want to hug her. I didn't even know this woman. Why was everything so awkward? Instead,

I lifted my chin. "Hello, May. It's nice to meet you. Lake says only good things."

There, smooth. Not really. Zach began to move out of frame, with Lake at his side as the two went to speak to the hostess, leaving May and me alone.

This wasn't going to be awkward at all.

The woman just smiled at me, her eyes wide. "It's nice to meet you, too. And Lake does speak highly of you. Also, this is very awkward, so I'm so sorry if I say something stupid. I know that your cousin said that I should be set up with you which is great but I'm not great at blind dates and apparently this is a double date and now I'm going to stop talking." She said the words so quickly they all ran into one breath.

I shook my head and laughed. "We're on the same page there."

"Okay, good. It's nice to meet you, Leif Montgomery."

"And it's nice to meet you too, May."

We made our way to Lake and Zach, who had gotten our table, and we all sat down, talking about work and other things. May was in child life development, taught online classes, and was also a nanny.

"I'm actually about to start with a new family soon. I'm excited. I know that being a nanny isn't something that most people strive for, or at least that's what they tell you, but I love being able to work with children and be the person that is there when a single parent or even both parents are out in the workforce, trying to do everything."

I nodded, taking a sip of my beer. "I get you completely. With how my parents worked, I was lucky that they were able to get childcare within the buildings. Since they each owned their own businesses, they made it work. But my family worked long hours, and that's why I ended up being the babysitter a lot of the times when childcare wasn't an option." I cleared my throat. "I'm a lot older than a lot of my cousins," I added.

"Both of us are, but I'm glad that you only said yourself," Lake said, grinning. She leaned into Zach as she spoke, the four of us in a horseshoe-shaped booth. That gave May and me space since this was a first date and still awkward as hell, and so Lake and Zach could cuddle. Not that that was something I needed to be a part of.

"Oh, I'm glad that you didn't judge. The last few dates that I've been on they always gave me weird looks because I think they expected a nanny to be this old crone or someone that's looking for a different job." She shrugged and continued. "When

I eventually get married and maybe even start a family, I want to continue my job. I like being there to help another family achieve their goals. And I can't believe I just said start a family on my first date. And that I mentioned that I've been on a few other dates." She let out a breath. "I'm notoriously bad at dating. Like, the worst. Just warning you."

I laughed, shaking my head. "I'm rusty at it, so don't worry." And even though I said that, I had a feeling that May felt no spark towards me, and I didn't feel anything towards her. She was nice and pleasant, and I could probably consider her a friend one day. But there wasn't any spark. May's eyes weren't dancing. She wasn't leaning forward, trying to touch my hand across the table. We were just sitting there casually, enjoying a really good steak, as Lake and Zach enjoyed their date.

By the end of dinner, I didn't want dessert, and neither did May, so we said goodbye to the other couple, who decided to stay. I walked May to her car, ignoring Lake's warning look, but I didn't know what exactly she was warning me about.

"Thanks for dinner," May said. "I could have paid. I know this is a blind date and all that, but you didn't have to pay."

I shook my head. "I paid for the four of us

because I wanted to be nice. I'll make Lake pay next time."

May beamed. "Yes, I like that. You guys are a good family."

"Anyway," I said, clearing my throat as I stuck my hands in my pockets. "I guess I'll see you around."

May just looked at me, threw her head back, and laughed. "You're right. You are rusty at this."

"Sorry." Heat flushed my skin, and I resisted the urge to tug on my eyebrow ring.

"It's okay. No spark. I'm used to it. I don't spark well."

"May, I'm sorry." I cringed. "It's not you."

"Oh, God, please don't say that. 'It's not you. It's me. You're working on yourself. You're just so busy with work.' I've heard it all."

"Seriously?" I asked. May was hot. Nice, but there just wasn't a spark.

She shrugged. "It's okay. I'll probably see you around sometime because I am friends with Lake. However, I am perfectly fine having this be our one and only. You'll find your person. It's okay that it's not me." And with that, she got in the car and left, leaving me standing there.

Well then. Tonight wasn't horrible, but it wasn't

great. I got in my car, and instead of heading home where I'd be alone, watching something on some streaming service while I drank a beer and pretended that I knew what I was doing with my life, I headed into Montgomery Ink Legacy.

We were the third branch of the company and the first owned by our generation. Montgomery Ink was the tattoo shop in downtown Denver. While there were open spots for some walk-ins and special circumstances, my father, aunt, and their team had years' worth of waiting lists. They worked their asses off and made sure to get in everybody that they could, but people wanted Austin Montgomery's art. Same with my aunt, Maya.

There was another tattoo shop down in Colorado Springs, owned by my parents' cousins, who I just called aunt and uncle because we were close enough that using real titles for everybody got confusing. Montgomery Ink Too was thriving down there, and they had waiting lists as well. My family could have opened more shops and gone nation-wide, even global if they wanted to, but they liked keeping it how it was, in the family and those connected.

We were a branch, but our own in the making. I had gone into business with Lake, of course, and

Sebastian, when he was ready, as well as Nick. Nick was my best friend. I had known him for ages, and he had wanted to be part of something as well. He might not be a Montgomery by name, but he had eaten over at my family's house enough times throughout the years that he was practically a Montgomery. And he had invested in the company as well, and so now we were nearly a year into owning the shop and trying not to fail.

I pulled into the parking lot, grateful it was still open since we didn't close until nine most nights, and greeted Nick, who was still working.

Sebastian was in the back, going over sketches with a client, and I nodded at him. He might be eighteen, but he was still in training, an apprentice, and was working his ass off to learn.

"Date sucked then?" Sebastian asked, and Nick just rolled his eyes and went back to work on a client's wrist.

"I don't want to talk about it," I groaned.

The rest of the staff was off since Nick would close up on his own. Sebastian was just there since he didn't have homework or a date with Marley.

"Was she hot at least?" Sebastian asked, and the client, a woman in her sixties, bopped him on the head with her bag gently.

"Sebastian Montgomery. Be nice."

Sebastian blushed. "Sorry, Mrs. Anderson."

I looked over at the woman and grinned. "Hi, Mrs. Anderson. It's nice to see you out of the classroom."

She narrowed her eyes at me, even though they filled with laughter. "I needed my next Jane Austen tattoo, thank you very much," the older woman said as she went back to working with Sebastian. She had been my and then Sebastian's English teacher. The fact that she was on her fifth tattoo with some literary quote told me that I had been damn lucky in most of my teachers growing up.

She was kick-ass, and I had a feeling that she would let Sebastian do the tattoo for her rather than just have him work on the design with me as we did for most of the people who came in. He had learned under my father and was working under me now. It was strange to think that he wasn't a little kid anymore. But he was in a long-term relationship, kicking ass in college, and knew what he wanted to do with his life.

I might know what I want to do with my work life, but everything else seemed a little off.

"So it didn't work out?" Nick asked as he

walked up to the front desk with the clients after going over aftercare.

"Not really," I said, looking down at my phone.

The client, a woman in her mid-twenties with bright pink hair, a lip ring, and kind eyes, leaned over the desk to look at me.

"You'll find someone, Leif. Don't worry."

I looked at our regular and shook my head. "Thanks, Kim. Too bad that you don't swing this way."

I winked as I said it, a familiar refrain from both of us.

Kim was married to a woman named Sonya, and the two of them were happy and working on in vitro with donated sperm for their first kid.

"Hey, I'm sorry too that I'm a lesbian. I'll never know what it means to have Leif Montgomery. Or any Montgomery, since I found my love far too quickly. I mean, what am I ever going to do not knowing the love of a Montgomery?"

Mrs. Anderson chuckled from her chair, Sebastian held back a snort, and I just looked at Nick, who rolled his eyes and helped Kim out of the place.

I was tired, but it was okay. The date wasn't all bad. May was nice. But it felt like I didn't have much right then.

And then Nick sat in front of me, scowled, and I realized that I did have something. I had my friends and my family. I didn't need much more.

"So, you and May didn't work out?"

I raised a brow. "You knew her name? Did I tell you that?"

Nick shook his head. "Lake did."

That made sense, considering the two of them spoke as much as we did. "So, was it your idea to set me up on a blind date?"

"Fuck no. That was all Lake. I just do what she says. Like we all do."

I sighed and went through my appointments for the next day. "We're busy for the next month. That's good, right?" I asked.

"You're the business genius here. I just play with ink. But yes, that's good. Now, don't let your cousin set you up any more dates. Find them for yourself. You know what you're doing."

"So says the man who dates less than me."

"That's what you think. I'm more private about it. As it should be." I flipped him off as he stood up, then he gestured towards a stack of bills in the corner. "You have a few personal things that made their way here. Don't want you to miss out on them before you head home."

"Thanks, bro."

"No problem. I'm going to help Sebastian with his consult, and then I'll clean up. You should head home. Though you're doing it alone, so I feel sorry for you."

"Fuck you," I called out.

"Fuck you, too."

"Boys," Mrs. Anderson said, in that familiar English teacher refrain, and both Nick and I cringed before saying, "Sorry," simultaneously.

Sebastian snickered, then went back to work, and I headed towards the edge of the counter, picking up the stack of papers. Most were bills, some were random papers that needed to be filed or looked over. Some were just junk mail. But there was one letter, written in block print that didn't look familiar. Chills went up my spine and I opened it, wondering what the fuck this was. Maybe it was someone asking to buy my house. I got a lot of handwritten letters for that, but I didn't think this was going to be that. I swallowed hard, slid open the paper, and froze.

"I'll find you, boy. Oops. Looks like I already did. Be waiting. I know you miss me."

I let the paper hit the top of the counter and

swallowed hard, trying to remain cool so I didn't worry anyone else.

I didn't know exactly who that was from, but I had a horrible feeling that they wouldn't wait long to tell me.

Read the rest in Bittersweet Promises!
OUT NOW!

wait to see what comes next with the new generation, the Talons. Keep them coming, Carrie Ann!" – Lara Adrian, New York Times bestselling author of CRAVE THE NIGHT

"With snarky humor, sizzling love scenes, and brilliant, imaginative worldbuilding, The Dante's Circle series reads as if Carrie Ann Ryan peeked at my personal wish list!" – NYT Bestselling Author, Larissa Ione

"Carrie Ann Ryan writes sexy shifters in a world full of passionate happily-ever-afters." – *New York Times* Bestselling Author Vivian Arend

"Carrie Ann's books are sexy with characters you can't help but love from page one. They are heat and heart blended to perfection." *New York Times* Bestselling Author Jayne Rylon

Carrie Ann Ryan's books are wickedly funny and deliciously hot, with plenty of twists to keep you guessing. They'll keep you up all night!" USA Today Bestselling Author Cari Quinn

"Once again, Carrie Ann Ryan knocks the Dante's Circle series out of the park. The queen of hot, sexy, enthralling paranormal romance, Carrie Ann is an author not to miss!" *New York Times* bestselling Author Marie Harte

ACKNOWLEDGMENTS

With every book comes a new way to say thank you to those I adore the most. I couldn't do this without my team and they know it.

So thank you Team Carrie Ann for being here. You know who you are. I literally couldn't not write these books and find these characters without you.

And thank you dear reader, for still being here after all this time.

xoxo,
Carrie Ann

About the Author

Carrie Ann Ryan is the New York Times and USA Today bestselling author of contemporary, paranormal, and young adult romance. Her works include the Montgomery Ink, Redwood Pack, Fractured Connections, and Elements of Five series, which have sold over 3.0 million books worldwide. She started writing while in graduate school for her advanced degree in chemistry and hasn't stopped since. Carrie Ann has written over seventy-five novels and novellas with more in the works. When she's not losing herself in her emotional and action-packed worlds, she's reading as much as she can while wrangling her clowder of cats who have more followers than she does.